Eva's GIFT

KELLY L. HOWARTH

EVA'S GIFT
ISBN 978-1-7753154-6-9 (Print)
ISBN 978-1-7753154-7-6 (Digital)

Cover design by Eswari Kamireddy
Interior layout by Eswari Kamireddy
Author image by Walmart Canada

Betrayal is the only truth that sticks.
-Arthur Miller

Acknowledgements

Thank you to my husband, Luigi Perrotta, who supports me and gives me the space to muse and write.

I am so grateful for my Fiverr layout artist, Eswari Kamireddy, who captured the essence of the story to create a lovely cover and book design.

A skilled editor helps the author transcend the story to let its characters lead—through coaching and educating. I am incredibly grateful for my Editor, Claudia Del Balso, whose thoughtful developmental and substantive edits of *Eva's Gift* kept me at the forefront of my writing.

Many thanks to those who agreed to read and contribute their ideas about *Eva's Gift*'s multiple drafts and stages:

- My friend Rebecca O'Kill asked helpful questions about the characters; she suggested early edits that shaped the story.
- My friend Anne-Marie Rousseau, Psychiatrist

and Artist, gave precise feedback about the characters' motivations, which was critical for their development.

- My supportive brother, Brent Howarth, was adamant that certain scenes remained in the book and cheered me on in writing fiction.

Thank you to my nephew, Andrew Howarth, who gave valuable feedback about the time and setting elements. Andrew co-produced the *Eva's Gift* book trailer with me—I am grateful for his creative video production and editing skills!

Contents

Prologue

"You hold it like this. See? Not too tight," Isabella places Eva's hands at ten and two on the steering wheel. She is teaching her younger sister how to drive.

"And you always keep your focus on the road ahead. Check your side and rearview mirrors often. Remember Eva, things are always closer than they appear," Isabella warns.

"Kind of like family," seventeen-year-old Eva muses.

Isabella smirks because she understands the irony. She and Eva share a unique bond. As children, they helped each other deal with complex family dynamics. And Isabella doesn't take Eva's generosity for granted.

"Yes. You can control the car, but you can't control everything around you—like the other drivers. They sometimes come out of nowhere. And they do stupid things. One mistake can change a person's life," Isabella is wise beyond her twenty-two years.

"Bella, enough with the doom and gloom. Let's do this!" Eva is eager to begin.

Isabella's new white 2010 Nissan, her university graduation gift from her dad, crawls from the mall parking space. The empty lot serves as Eva's blank canvas for practice.

One

Jessica

Jessica turns the key, listening for the familiar cough. But she hears a choke. Her first car, a ruby red 1982 Honda Civic, was a present from doting parents to their only child as Jessica graduated with honours when she obtained her bachelor's degree. The car needs servicing, and Jessica is negligent in finding the time with all her deadlines. "Damn it—not again!" she cries, "They say bad things come in threes—what's next?!" Jessica grips the steering wheel and shakes it as if to awaken her car.

Jessica cannot be late for this presentation on the Kessler account. Five of her company's top clients, who look more like her grandfather's buddies ready to play dominoes, will gather around the oval mahogany table in the conference room. Jessica will display the craftiness with which she sells them her dream for their crystal empire, from marketing plan to public relations strategy. The pinched sagging faces will 'ooh' and 'ahh' over her vision board and PowerPoint presentation with voiceover, describing how the project could launch their fine crystals to an international market. Jessica never failed them in their other ventures; these veterans are forever seeking their next business high.

Jessica's imagination runs rampant; her hand stops trying to coax the sputtering engine. At this hour, the tell-tale Diamond Taxicabs are cruising the main artery of her Montreal borough, Notre-Dame-de-Grace, seeking their first fare. She decides to take a taxi.

Today is Friday: presentation, lunchtime workout, then off to a gynecology appointment this afternoon to renew her birth control pills. Jessica feels disappointed that her period came this month despite missing two pills mid-cycle. Although she isn't seeing anyone seriously, Jessica has casual sex dalliances. Her mind is in the overdrive her car lacks during her five-minute walk to de Maisonneuve Boulevard West.

My early thirties suck! Jessica laments. This age is a netherworld: she's too old to have snagged the up-and-coming lawyer after finishing her master's studies and too young to consider herself a spinster. *Oh, but a baby daddy would be lovely!* Jessica's thoughts run away as she fantasizes about a babe in arms—smiling and cooing at her.

She remembers her mother's adage during her teenage years: "Men are babies—just bigger and needier!" Jessica's mom ran a smooth home despite her thriving career, often without help from her husband. And his complaining was typical when he'd catch a common cold!

Who has the time for both a child and a kid? Jessica concedes that she needs a man anyway, if not for a loving relationship, at least as a sperm donor. *A family man would be ideal!* Jessica cannot let go of her dream, the one hammered into her by her parents: the adoring husband, a beautifully appointed home, and two-and-a-half children, preferably a boy and a girl. *Isn't that what all women want? Isn't that what she should have by now?*

Jessica engages in fleeting relationships that never surpass the honeymoon phase. She does all the right things. She wears lacy lingerie, a come-hither look in her eyes, melting men on the spot as they fumble with minuscule fasteners for entry into the maze of these expensive, delicate threads. They are frustrated by how this apparel works—or does not work for them. These horny men, used to mechanics and fixing things, become idiots around a piece of lace with minute hooks embedded in their pattern. Jessica enjoys watching them struggle, knowing they eventually land the prize and feel gratified.

Jessica feels self-satisfaction about her ability to

reduce these powerful men to soft putty in her hands. She wonders if there's a difference between pleasure and punishment. But Jessica wants more than those fleeting encounters. She wants a life now, one to call her own. She wants what her friends all obtained years ago, what her colleagues and fellow gym rats have: solid men, children, and families. Jessica feels a bitter taste crawling up her throat, spreading to her tongue. She is ready for *her* prize.

"Going into the city?" the gum-snapping female cabbie slows down on her side, waking Jessica from her reverie.

"Yes!" Jessica hops in and rearranges her black skirt. She tucks her red scarf into the top v of her coat. Her 'knock-them-dead suit,' as her best friend, Cassie, calls it, Jessica wears this lucky power suit to make a public relations pitch. Tugging at the top of her slipping stay-up hose, Jessica reckons it won't be lost on these old geezers. She makes a mental note to buy garters at Simon's this afternoon. Garters? *Do they still exist?* She will find an alternative to these stockings that seem to fall faster than most men she seduces.

Jessica guesses her problem: *The good ones are already taken.* She needs to set her sights a little lower. Jessica sighs, leaning back into the hard leather seat and closing her eyes. As the cab wends through the dense Montreal traffic, she contemplates looking for an older man.

Jessica knows she will arrive on time, never disappointing the senior men whose drivers deliver them right to the door of the tall glass building that houses her uncle's public relations firm twenty floors up. Afraid of heights, Jessica's heart jumps into her throat every time she steps too close to a window; its bowed effect makes her queasy stomach contract when she sees the traffic moving below.

Jessica jolts from her reverie and sprints from the cab, catching her stiletto in a sidewalk grate. Her knee grazes the pavement, snagging her hose. "Shit!" she exclaims and rights herself, inches from the spinning revolving door, noticing the run snaking up her thigh. *Damn stockings! Strike two! What will number three be? Hopefully not at the meeting.* Jessica pats her skirt, jostles her handbag and business tote, and comes to a complete stop as the revolving door opens past her. *Close call!* She quips and waits for the next opportunity to move to the inner sanctum of this familiar building.

As soon as she could legally work, Jessica became a summer intern. She loved the business, and it had shaped her university major. Then Jessica became a permanent employee five years ago, opting to complete a Master of Business Administration at night. Jessica graduated with distinction in 1991, as the Internet Explosion was about to revolutionize how she delivered her public relations pitches.

Jessica was a whiz kid; she surfaced as a leader on

class projects, and classmates sought her insights and opinions. Her father's brother had waited for her to graduate, seeking young, fresh talent with innovative ideas. Uncle Francis told her she was what the firm needed when more senior staff were retiring. Jessica was chomping at the bit, ready to integrate the recent technology with her minted diploma; she wanted to roll up her sleeves with those accounts lying dormant while employees bided their time to collect their pensions.

Francis had handed Jessica the Kessler account with their older pinch-faced men, who appeared ominous and challenging to please. With her light strawberry blonde hair and green eyes, this new kid on the block caught their attention. They immediately loved Jessica's refreshing approach.

"The eyes did it for them," Francis later told her. Jessica laughed it off; she preferred believing that her astuteness and professionalism sold them that she was the best person to push their ideas to fruition. *She could tell the old geezers to paint their car purple and place a spinning crystal ball on the top, and they would! Trust is an attractive building block.*

Jessica has enough time to peel off her damaged stockings and retrieve the vision board exhibit beside her filing cabinet. The computer screen would be connected to a projector, ready to amaze her audience with her unique ideas. Her late-night hours deliberating over different scenarios means she is well-prepared for these men's discerning intellects. Their voices waft down the hall from the elegant conference room. She plans to breeze in and wow them with her exhibits. *Not so tough a job for a Friday morning!*

Two

Irini and Paul

"Hey Paul, would you please pick up my suit at the dry cleaners on your way home from work? My reading is Monday morning at the library." Irini's lazy voice trails off as she rolls over to sleep longer. Bella had woken up around two a.m. from a nightmare, stirring the whole house. They all went back to sleep as a delirious Irini trudged along the upstairs hallway, rocking Isabella. The babysitter had been off for the week, so they were on their own. Paul's days are intense; Irini does not expect him to soothe their little one back to sleep.

"And what's in it for me?" Paul asks.

"A happy wife," Irini closes her eyes, leaving Paul to grope in the dark for his clothes. Their two oldest children are still in bed because today is a pedagogical day.

There is no morning routine to navigate this day. Life has been hectic lately in their sprawling suburban home on the West Island that hugs the outskirts of Montreal. Their house runs like a well-oiled machine. Paul usually breakfasts with their children, letting Irini sleep off the middle-of-the-night waking of a toddler who still does not sleep through her nights. Isabella awakens once the kids go their separate ways to elementary and high school, and Irini starts the daily routine again; she cannot seem to catch up on her sleep.

The youngest member of the Caldwell family needs time and attention at a point when both their careers are peaking. Irini's writing career enables flexibility and a work-life blend as an established author.

As an infant, Isabella slept for hours at a time, allowing Irini long delicious stretches to write. During her toddler years, she would play by herself on the floor at Irini's feet. The words would tumble onto the page, the keyboard clicking in unison with the office fireplace mantle clock ticking. Minutes would melt into hours. Now, with her fourth birthday in sight, Isabella is a precocious child, keen to explore her environment and no longer content to stick to the confines of Irini's writing space. So, Irini snatches opportunities when she can, carving blocks of time when the babysitter keeps Isabella occupied.

Irini had been battling fibromyalgia for the past five years, undiagnosed until a concerned associate introduced his physician wife at a cocktail party. Because the symptoms coincided with Isabella's arrival and night-waking, Irini had chalked it up to the challenges of being an older mom. With limited reserves, Irini's pain and irritability belie a more severe condition requiring long rest periods when she is not writing. Of course, she always must make time for three weekly workouts, along with daily yoga classes—movement significantly improves her struggle with the widespread pain that causes sleep problems, fatigue, and emotional distress.

Paul's lips graze his sleeping wife's forehead, damp with sweat. He turns off the dim lamp and exits the bedroom. Irini looks so good lying there, all cozy, that Paul wants to crawl back into bed and make slow love to the woman with whom he has shared the better half of his adult life. His forties have been kind to him, but his impending fifties might not be so forgiving. If only Paul felt the sex drive of his younger self. *Life gets in the way.* Paul thinks as he tiptoes down the stairs to a quiet, tidy kitchen to make a smoothie.

Paul is a junior partner and new to the Kessler account, following the lead of his older mentors. A quick check of his watch tells him he must leave now to avoid the snaking line of cars headed into the city—sweat beads on his forehead at the thought of fighting traffic. Paul doesn't have the same luxury of a driver as his partners, these filthy rich men who are short on time.

Loosening his tie, he feels like a pressure-cooker, although they had pre-approved a watered-down version of today's presentation. The partners will relax as the final submission unfolds.

Today there will be exceptional learning about how all the pieces fit together to push the consortium of companies further up the food chain. Kessler will do well as the lead for the group of companies. It will view the pitch and consider all the costs and angles. Paul could relax as his role is that of a voyeur—this time around.

Three

Jessica

Heat crawls up Jessica's spine, tingling and making its way around her throat, closing in like a snake choking its victim. Her face flushes with shyness. Jessica rarely reacts this way when facing the old pinch-faced men. But today is different! The men sit smiling around the vast oval mahogany table, except here among them is a new face: Paul Caldwell, introduced by the most senior man. Younger, fitter, with a hint of gray in his facial hair, his sandy blond mane wisps across his forehead, framing the bluest penetrating eyes.

Jessica averts her gaze, noting those eyes following her torso down the length of her legs—her bare legs! The heat starts ravaging her body. She reaches for her ice water, a pitcher placed at her spot courtesy of her trusted assistant Melissa, still hovering for any last-minute instructions. Melissa glances at Jessica, her eyes speaking what she cannot verbalize.

Paul is not the typical *Gentleman's Quarterly Magazine* handsome; he carries himself distinguishably. She notices Paul's resemblance to Richard Branson, the CEO of the Virgin Group. *He's not even my type. He's well-bred, though.* Jessica determines as the sunlight catches his bejewelled left hand in a prism.

The heat turns ice-cold; Jessica feels relieved knowing this man is married. No doubt he even has children close to her age. *Focus, Jess*, she reminds herself. *Damn, Murphy's Law is making the presentation challenging!* Jessica has been working hard these past weeks, juggling three high-priority accounts. She wants to breeze through her pitch and start her weekend.

Jessica clears her parched throat to speak. All eyes watch, and she wishes she were a particle in the beaming sunlight. "Gentlemen…," Jessica begins, regaining her composure. The computer screen comes to life. Jessica hears the rest of her introduction as though she is looking down at someone else delivering her pitch.

The wall at the head of the conference table lights up with vivid images, and the room fills with sound. She can relax now that the slideshow is running. Jessica anticipates the questions following this fifteen-minute song and dance. In the meantime, she can study the expectant faces around the table for signs of approval.

They are impressed! Jessica focuses everywhere except on Paul with his rugged features. While she cannot read his reaction regarding her presentation, Jessica feels the scrutiny of this new younger member on her skin. While scanning the older men's faces, Jessica locks eyes with Paul. She quickly averts her gaze, flushing down to her chest. *This is so strange.* Jessica has never experienced sexual tension while presenting a pitch.

The video ends in the blink of an eye. Lights up by her assistant, Jessica is on her stilettoed feet, grabbing her vision board to reiterate the plan. She observes the smiles around the table—except for Paul. Jessica feels lost in the discomfort of him sizing her up. Paul's gaze fixes on her. *What is he thinking?*

Questions about the video presentation swirl around her faster than Jessica can keep up. She fights to compose herself. *It feels so intense!*

The most intimidating question comes from Paul: "What is it that you do in your spare time, again?" *Has Paul just asked a question about her personal life?!* It feels like something has pushed Jessica into the wall.

Jessica recovers with a comeback: "I look out at the Montreal skyline from my rooftop garden to gain inspiration about how to make Kessler Corporation a *tour de force* amongst its competitors." She smiles, taps the vision board, and continues to explain the crisp images. Jessica captures the group's collective imagination.

The elders stifle their laughter and nod in agreement.

Her response satisfies Paul as it nipped the challenge while maintaining his dignity. Jessica has preserved her integrity.

Let's see how much virtue I have over drinks with this one later! Jessica allows herself a moment to fantasize while the vision board changes hands amidst satisfied "Oohs" and "Ahs." Arriving in Paul's grip, the board remains for a long time, his study of it a little more than the casual or cursory glances of the pinched-faced men. Jessica worries he is scrutinizing it. *Paul will no doubt ask more questions!* Jessica braces herself for the onslaught, which never comes.

She finishes her presentation and watches the men rise, a cacophony of voices and approval erupting as they come forward, shake her hand, and pat her on the back. Francis enters the room to witness them sealing the deal. Yet another coup for Imperial Media! Francis beams at Jessica as the men file out, all except Paul.

"What a superb presentation you gave!" Paul exclaims.

So flattering! Jessica beams.

"May I use your conference room to return some calls?" Paul's smile is beguiling.

Francis and Jessica reply, "Yes." in unison as Jessica gathers her papers. She hears Paul's calm voice on his cell phone as she beelines to her office down the hall and closes the door.

Standing out of sight of the sidelights, Jessica leans

against the door. She sighs with relief and closes her eyes: "What just happened in there?" Jessica whispers to herself. Then she feels a soft knock on her back. Melissa is checking in as she regularly does after these presentations. And Jessica is ready to compare notes about this up-and-comer, Paul Caldwell.

She whisks open her office door. Paul stands there, confident. "Did you forget something, or are you lost? Let me show you the way out," Jessica moves to lead him to the reception area.

"Neither. I can't easily forget a whip-smart woman like you," Paul grins, dimples etching the corners of his mouth.

Jessica raises her eyebrows. Paul replies: "Can I come in for a quick chat?"

"Sure," Jessica waves Paul to a chair at the mini-conference table beside her desk. She learned in business school not to let someone into her office because she wouldn't have the option to leave. This time management tip came from an expert. *What do they know anyway? Are they familiar with men like Paul?* Jessica scoffs that she is even thinking about 'a man like Paul.'

"Great presentation! Are you always on top of your game?" His ocean blue eyes light up.

"Always on top…of my game." Jessica doesn't blush.

"You made a bunch of elderly men proud. Consider how proud a younger one like me was?" Paul leans toward Jessica.

"I can imagine." Jessica retorts. *Oh, where was this chat laced with innuendo going?!*

Paul scans the interior of Jessica's office, taking in the stark décor. He notes the absence of family photographs. *So, she doesn't look married.* Above her L-shaped desk, a bulletin board holds a dozen post-it notes and a To-Do List. His eyes travel around the room and stop on the one thing out of place: a gnarled black nest of nylon stockings on the floor.

Jessica follows Paul's gaze and meets his raised eyebrows. She smiles demurely and says: "You didn't come here to inspect my office."

Uh, no. I came here to learn more about you. Paul thinks on his feet, but he cannot be so obvious. "I thought we could discuss the account a little more," Paul's excuse is lame, even to his ears.

"Your senior colleague told me he'd be in touch next week," Jessica reminds Paul.

"Let me take you to lunch…or we could have dinner," Paul persists, "What do you say, Jess?" Paul takes the liberty of creating familiarity to try to entice her.

"Only my best friend Cassie calls me that," Jessica rises from the conference table. She looks at her wrist: "My watch tells me it's time to end this chat with an older married man."

Older—ouch! Paul's mouth opens and closes as if to say something, then he holds his bare left hand out. He is overconfident.

Jessica could swear that what she saw glinting in the ray of sunlight was a wedding ring, one with a tiny single diamond. Jessica surmises that men rarely wear more than a gold band if they wear one—this ring had a stone.

Then she sees the gold cufflinks peeking from Paul's sleeves. *Was her mind playing tricks on her earlier, wanting it to be a wedding band, so she doesn't end up in another relationship that leads nowhere?* Jessica feels confused, and she thinks Paul is lying.

"What time do you finish work today?" Paul redirects Jessica's mind chatter.

"Lunchtime," she says, "I have an appointment this afternoon and won't be back." Jessica decides to play it cool with Paul.

"Ah, an early weekend. What time does your appointment finish?" Paul asks, "Or is it a date?" He is smug, thinking back to the lines he used to snag an unsuspecting Irini and casual sex partners since.

"Mid-afternoon—2:30," Jessica says. *Why was she telling this stranger?*

"Good, I'll pick you up at 2:30, and we can go for a late lunch, talk a bit, see where that takes us, then we can go for dinner." Paul is planning her evening!

"I have lunch plans. Dinner works better for me," Jessica likes Paul's persistence. He isn't wasting any time as most others had. She is not in the mood to waste time either. Jessica guesses that Paul is in his mid to late forties—not an impossible age gap and not old like her father—young enough to be serious about a relationship. An older man might be a welcome change of pace in her life.

"You'll give me the address. And I'll see you at 2:30," Paul smiles, satisfied.

Jessica scribbles the cross-street names on the back of her business card and hands it to Paul. *He could be the ONE. Might his swimmers be a good match for my eggs?* Jessica wonders.

Four

Irini

Like a blank page, the day stretches before Irini. The children are playing in the backyard. Their rescue dog, Roxie, a mix of brown and white, races around the girls, nipping at heels and delighting in their squeals. Jenn, Selena, and Isabella are engaged in a game of tag that involves hide-and-seek. Their beloved pet gives up their hiding spots, creating loud laughter. *Such a luxury that the siblings are spending time together! It rarely happens in this household, with everyone running their separate ways.* Irini wraps her fuzzy L.L. Bean sweater tighter around her slight frame and picks up her steaming mug of coffee in her cold hands, interlacing her fingers around it—they feel chilled.

Long wisps of streaked blonde hair fall into Inini's

brown eyes as she watches the threesome through the patio door. She smiles, grateful all is well in her world. Irini turns to trudge up to her attic office, where she will write for three hours before lunch, then do an activity with the girls until Paul returns from work—if he comes home.

♦ ♦ ♦

The day is zipping by, and Irini wants to create an experience for her children, so she decides to take them to the local lake with a beach: Cap Saint Jacques. She had hoped Paul would start his weekend early and join them for this family outing. Unless she hears from him, she expects he'll be occupied with meetings late into the day. Although it is Friday, it might as well be any other weekday evening. *It's tough not to feel resentful.* Irini understands that Paul is peaking in his success and needs the space to build on his professional reputation—requiring that he attend long-running last-minute meetings. Paul has long periods where a flurry of activity consumes his evenings and weekends, and he is frequently absent from home. Irini has noticed a pattern over the past five years.

Put pen to paper, Irini orders herself to her writing, despite the gnawing unsettled feeling in the pit of her stomach. She feels tired and restless; it must be the lack of sleep last night.

After years of writing and selling novels, Irini decided to try her hand at something more personal. This time, she tackles a memoir to shed light on her life. Not one to introspect, Irini feels her mid-forties are the perfect time to explore the threads weaving the tapestry of her existence.

Men buy red sports cars and have affairs; women start new careers. What a stereotypical thought! Irini catches herself musing. *What makes her expect other people will want to read about her family?* Irini intends to use her journey to help others. She decides that this work in progress is not about the final product but about the catharsis in drafting her story.

Five

Katerina

The garden was bursting with the vibrant colours and delicious fragrances of herbs and vegetables; their bounty would be impressive this season. Katerina was helping her mother pick the ripest tomatoes for canning. Mamo would make enough preserves to sustain them over the long, frigid winter, and they would sell the rest of their homemade fare at the local market. Katerina's favourite part of the harvest was negotiating with customers, knowing their labour had fetched the best price.

"Only the plump ones," Mamo directed as Katerina's two younger siblings ran through the garden squealing, delighting in the last days of summer despite the distant shelling. They were playing tag, and Mamo was shooing them out of the tender plants: "You'll trample our food! And then what will we eat? Go play over there!" she ordered.

Katerina hummed to block out the noises of war reverberating from outlying towns: air raid sirens and bombing. The ominous sounds were a sharp contrast to the idyllic scene in their garden as the tight-knit family was trying to live with normalcy in a cottage tucked amongst other homes on the outskirts of Krakow, Poland.

Tata, Katerina's dad, was still going to work on the assembly line at a munitions factory—at least he was employed during these unpredictable times. "It's because of the war that I have a job and can put food on the table," he reassured them.

◆ ◆ ◆

The garden was still growing when the foot traffic of invading soldiers squashed the bright tomatoes to a pungent mush rotting in the late-summer sun. Mamo herded the three siblings into the house and down to the damp basement to hide while Tata faced the enemy, trying to distract the soldiers from entering their home.

"We're not the enemy. Wyjdz! Leave now!" Katerina's father stood up to the invaders. He turned to walk into his home.

As Tata opened the door, one soldier shot his foot. Tata managed to limp across the threshold, lock the door, and join his family hiding in the cellar before the soldiers bashed their way inside the house.

The intruders looted alcohol and valuables. The family listened to the rustling in the pantry above their heads. These brutes were ravenous beasts that hadn't eaten for days!

Tata held a finger to his lips, silencing them while wincing with pain as Mamo tended his wounded foot like she was preparing a soft tomato. The children stayed quiet. Mamo and Tata felt they had a reprieve.

The undaunted soldiers wanted to achieve their sole purpose: kill innocent civilians and weaken the spirit of Poland. After their fill of food, the brutish soldiers left—except for one rebel emboldened by drink. He destroyed the cellar door and entered the dark space, using a pocket flashlight to illuminate his prey.

◆ ◆ ◆

Katerina awoke to the drone and hum of tanks rolling by the shot-out basement windows. She lay twisted on the cold cement floor; she ached all over her slender frame, her body trembled, and she wanted to vomit. Katerina didn't know if the dried blood on her torn underwear was hers. All she felt was numbness in her vagina, her first sexual experience at seventeen forced upon her by a drunken rogue in combat fatigues while her parents and siblings lay dying mere feet away. They couldn't pull him off her. And she couldn't save them.

A violent tremor began shaking the house. Katerina stumbled up the basement stairs into the blinding sun that lit up her besieged community. She felt shattered and alone, standing almost naked in the decimated garden amidst the debris and rubble of the fallen houses around her.

An Italian soldier walked toward her; his eyes filled with empathy. He was young like her and had a gentle face not hardened by the war. He muttered something in English about the house falling, his wild gestures summoning Katerina away. When he extended his hand, Katerina flinched. She felt broken and ashamed. Then Gino said his name, and Katerina knew she had to trust this one with her life, which was spared.

Gino

One Man's War

She carried him in her womb for nine months
Birthing after a long, painful labour
She cuddled and coddled him
Measles, flu, scraped knees, schoolyard fights
First week away at scout camp

Letters home, phone calls home

Then she stepped back
Giving him a wide berth
Teen turmoil, first kiss, first lost love
The doubt of young adulthood
Off to the front line

Letters home, phone calls home

Now she waits and worries

Clutching her womb in memory
Heart contracting with pain
So many miles away is the child
She cannot cuddle or coddle
And she cannot step back

She awaits those letters, that phone call

For she put this child into the world
And nurtured him
Now one man's war
Threatens to take her child out

No more letters home; that phone call comes

Gino fingers the wrinkled parchment paper on which he'd written his most profound intimate thoughts and fears in a heartfelt poem. It was a tribute to his mother. When Gino was conscripted at eighteen, their conversation was difficult because his Italian mamma, prone to dramatics, sobbed and pleaded with him to dodge the draft.

"Ma, you know I can't," Gino felt sensitive to her pain and could only repeat what he'd been told at the Italian Army registration office: "Our country needs me."

"You're my only son, Gino. I can't bear to lose you," Mamma persisted, massive tears staining her red cheeks. "*Per favore, non lasciarmi sola*—your father left me for another woman—now you are leaving me for what? A man who started this war!" she implored.

Gino turned away; he couldn't bear to listen to his mother's begging when he knew he had no choice. His platoon was leaving the next day, and all Gino could do was pray.

Gino had not been able to enroll in university, instead opting to work after high school to support his mother and sister when his father took off with a local *puttana*, the town whore who made all the wives wary.

Gino loved sharing information with his friends—things he'd learned from various newspapers and journals. He wanted to study literature and become an English teacher or journalist. Instead, Gino ended up drafted into a war he'd vowed never to fight.

Combing through the newspaper, Gino noticed the bold headline calling all males over eighteen into the army. He took three days to process what he knew: they would come for him if he did not step up. A letter arrived the following week, directing Gino to the local recruiting office where he was rubber-stamped and issued his marching orders.

He would report to his command unit a fortnight later for basic training. An eighteen-year-old who was never allowed to play with toy guns as a child would be managing a loaded rifle—and was trained to aim and kill. While Gino thought that words held power, he was about to discover the power of a live weapon.

When he wasn't fighting on the front lines or digging fox holes to shelter from the enemy, Gino kept a diary detailing his horrifying experiences. Unable to sleep because he feared for his life, he'd write for hours into the night with a dim light on his pen, careful not to alert the enemy.

He tore the poem from his diary when the field commander found him writing: "Hey, Sissy, you're going to get us all killed with that stuff. Put it away!" he'd spat in Gino's face.

The sergeant grabbed the thin notebook and tore it down the spine. He threw the pages into the dirt and stepped on them with his combat boot as if grinding a lit cigarette into the ground. Gino vowed to be more cautious when writing as he tucked his thoughtful prose into his breast pocket. He later slipped the poem into a letter home to his mother, which he never mailed. *Was he foreshadowing his death?* Gino could not scare Mamma with his desperate thoughts, especially because she had objected to him fighting in this war.

Gino wanted to honour his mother's gift of life to him. So, if he came home in a body bag, the poem would tell Mamma what Gino had been too guilty to say before he left: he understood what she went through to give birth to and raise him, only to turn him over to a cruel warmonger.

Gino's parents reconciled during the war. They immigrated to Canada: "Let's try again. We can live a peaceful life in a land where people are free," Pa had assured Mamma. Despite her misgivings about taking back her cheating husband, she felt it was better to be safe in a peaceful country with a cheater than alone in an unstable country while he ran off with other women.

After four gruelling years, Gino joined his parents in Canada, and his letter made it into his mother's hands. She was so relieved that she scarcely read the profound words, for she kept hugging Gino and thanking God for his safe return. And she was excited to meet Katerina, his new bride, a happy by-product of her suffering—she would become a Nonna sooner than expected. Mamma passed down the tattered poem in a keepsake box to Katerina as part of her wedding gift to the new couple.

Physically unscathed except for a minor shrapnel wound, Gino was in denial that he was emotionally scarred by World War Two's constant fighting, killing, and carnage. He found a way to self-medicate and erase the brutal images that flashed their continuous reminder in his head. Gino no longer wanted to replay the horrific memories of the war and revisit the pain. He returned the frayed page of prose to the memorabilia tin, wiping a tear from his eye. He never wanted to open that box again.

Seven

Paul

Paul has two hours to wait for his date with Jessica. He had decided to skip the rest of his workday since it was Friday afternoon—an early start to a much-deserved weekend since he's been logging long hours on both the Kessler and Ralston accounts.

Paul decides to take a run; he retrieves the sports bag he'd checked at Imperial Media's reception, finds a bathroom, and changes into his sports clothes. Paul extracts his wedding ring from his jacket and places it into the inner zippered pocket of the bag. Irini would never forgive him if he lost it. She insisted on using the remainder of her student loan to purchase the band with its glinting diamond to complement the one Paul bought her. The thin ridge on the side of the ring cuts into Paul's finger while he writes with his left hand, so he often removes it, telling himself that is the only reason.

Paul places the bag in the trunk of his car before sprinting off down Sherbrooke Street towards Westmount Park. He considers how Jessica observed his ring. A wise girl like her does not second-guess herself. Paul appreciates Jessica's smarts, and he craves her body! He needs an infusion of youth these days. As fifty approaches, Paul is obsessed with his virility: *I work out, and women often look twice.* Paul's finances let him avail himself of all manner of personal care. Botox facial treatments have helped. Paul's vanity aims to preserve his fleeting youth.

At forty-six, Irini looks younger than ever, Paul deems. *Even with her illness and fatigue.* It feels challenging to keep up. Usually, the reverse is true, but the years have been kinder to her. Paul fights the stress of making and breaking deals in his company ventures in ways Irini, the consummate mother, will never understand. She has a tough lot raising three boisterous children while turning out novels and keeping up with book launches and signings, but as they often say, it is a jungle out there for Paul.

Paul provides well for his family and allows himself his little dalliances. He could not wait to see Jess; he pictures her bare legs wrapped around his torso. *Argh, the thought of it! Would she be seduced tonight?* He wonders as his feet pound through the park, filling with people starting their weekends. Paul juggles the portable music player, placing it in a holster around his hips, and positions his earphones; he silences them all, enjoying his fantasy about the evening ahead.

Paul's first taste of infidelity occurred with Irini's youngest sister, Cassandra, a seasoned seductress whom he could not resist. Paul had picked Cassandra up for a family gathering because her car was in the shop for servicing. He drove into his home's double garage and no sooner cut the engine when he found his body twisted into a pretzelled frenzy doing the deed with a willing Cassandra. It was hot, urgent, and heady, combined with the fear of being caught. As Irini entered to access their second refrigerator, Paul and Cassandra froze and ducked when lights flooded the garage. Then the phone rang, and Irini turned back into the house. *Narrow escape!*

Their fling had meant nothing to Paul, but it had confirmed his desirability, jumpstarting Paul's journey into appeasing a fragile ego seeking validation through sex.

During the summer of 1988, Cassandra showed up with a baby girl Paul suspected was the fruit of their hurried sex in the backseat of his cramped sports coupe. Avoiding Paul's eyes, Cassandra explained how this incident with a much older man, already settled and disinterested in anything more, devastated her lifestyle: "We discussed it," she lied. "He's not interested in starting over at his age. And I won't raise a kid alone," Cassandra implored Irini and Paul to take the baby because she was not a fit mother: "I'll sign over all parental rights and privileges," she assured them.

No behind-closed-doors discussion was necessary. Irini and Paul replied in unison: "Yes, of course." each for selfish reasons. Paul thought it was the least he could do given the presumed circumstances. He could see how Cassandra's willingness to forfeit her chance at motherhood tore at Irini, reminiscent of the pain of her conception.

Cassandra had called her 'Baby' for the month since her birth. Now, she looked to Irini and Paul for inspiration. They spent the rest of the afternoon discussing feeding schedules, routines, and other particulars Cassandra learned about her daughter by reading. Another escort had given her a dog-eared Dr. Benjamin Spock's *Baby and Childcare* book: "You'll need this," she'd told Cassandra. "Oh, no, I won't!" but Cassandra took it anyway. The guide lay at the bottom of her baby tote bag, and Cassandra was grateful that Irini would see she had at least tried.

"You've been nursing her, right, Cassandra?" Irini asked. She had breastfed her daughters until each was two years old.

"Not after the first few days. She had trouble latching onto my boob, and when I gave her the bottle, she took to it immediately! Who could blame her? It was so much easier!" Cassandra pulled a bottle out of her pink Gucci diaper bag and handed it to Irini. She felt relieved not to answer these plaintive cries for feeding anymore.

After the baby was fed and nestled amongst pillows in the corner of the sofa, Irini thought: *It would be best to give her a strong name like Isabella I of Castile, Europe's great queen regnant,* so she proposed 'Isabella.'

"We'll call her Bella for short," Irini further suggested.

Cassandra's eyes lit up: "Yes, for beautiful."

"Like her mother," Paul said, adding, "Both mothers."

Cassandra glanced at her sister, fishing for a reaction, wondering what Irini might do if she had any clue.

"Bella she is then!" Irini exclaimed, beaming.

Unbeknownst to either woman, this child would be the namesake of her prostitute grandmother.

"We can fetch the girls' baby furniture from the basement. Bella will stay in our room so I can wake up for her at night." Irini affirmed.

"Oh, thank you, Irini! I know Bella will grow up happy here with you and Paul!" Cassandra admitted she was relieved. She hadn't wanted the baby from the start, so she never bothered trying to bond with her.

Irini made short order of broaching the sensitive details of this new bounty in their lives. "You're still her mother," Irini reassured Cassandra despite her vehement protests. Cassandra reiterated that she would sign any legal documents to formalize the adoption: "Let's ask Gianni to draw up the papers," she said.

◆ ◆ ◆

Paul consults his watch; he must do a cool-down to make an excellent first impression before picking Jessica up at the agreed time. *He met her hours ago and felt like a teenage boy with a crush! But oh, she is gorgeous!* And young and vibrant and all the qualities disappearing with his fleeting youth. Paul decides to pick Jessica up on the way back from his jog.

Traffic clogs the downtown core as Paul pants and sweats his way up the hill to the address Jessica had scribbled on the reverse of her business card. He slows to a brisk walk and turns down the street, bumping into Jessica as she rounds the corner. She holds a spray of yellow daffodils, her favourite blooms.

"For me? Isn't it supposed to be the other way around?" Paul exclaims. He regrets that he had not thought to buy Jessica flowers himself. It had been a mere few hours since he first saw this gorgeous, talented woman: *Flowers would be too pretentious,* Paul reminds himself.

"Sorry, but these are for me!" Jessica explains, "I buy myself flowers every Friday to celebrate the end of the week. And I just love these spring blooms!"

"Ah, a ritual," Paul says, making a mental note to beat her to it next time.

"Kind of," her plump pink lips becoming a pout. Jessica doesn't say that she is worth it, that her hard work justifies seeing the beautiful bouquet on her dining table, and despite how awful things are going, she can look at the flowers and feel better. *And things didn't go as she had expected at her gynecologist appointment.* Jessica opens her mouth to say more but decides to leave it there. *Let Paul wonder.*

"All went well at your appointment?" Paul didn't want to pry as he tries to make conversation.

"Yes," Jessica would not elaborate on the intimate details of her gynecological health. Changing the subject, "Now that is an interesting outfit," Jessica refers to Paul's shorts and tee-shirt. She notes his long, muscled legs and how Paul's biceps flex, something she couldn't see under his tailored suit this morning. "You should have warned me. I don't follow casual Fridays."

"I went for a run while I waited for you. My clothes are in the car," Paul says.

"Ah, like Superman, you change in phone booths?" Jessica quips.

"When I must," Paul grins and winks.

No wonder the man is in such great shape! Jessica surmises.

Jessica is impatient; she usually buries herself in a novel she carries. It reminds Jessica of the long wait to see her doctor. Thankfully, the waiting room stocks popular magazines. She was grateful for last month's issue of *Cosmopolitan* as she had been too busy to buy it. This chick mag is her go-to, and Jessica relishes the self-scoring quizzes and informative articles about how to attract 'the One.'

Paul takes Jessica's elbow and guides her down the street to his car. *The faster, the better.* Paul doesn't want to bump into someone he knows. He plans to make a quick stop at his office to collect his files and change into his business attire, minus the tie. Paul will drive them to the South Shore to minimize his chances of meeting a colleague or acquaintance in the city. He is grateful that while Montreal is a prominent hub, his wife keeps to the West Island where they live because it has all the shopping and amenities their family needs.

"Here we are," Paul opens the passenger door of his Audi Coupe with the convenient tinted windows and hurries to the driver's side.

"A true gentleman," Jessica loves Paul's chivalry. "Thank you!"

Paul feels appreciated. "You are most welcome, Mademoiselle."

"And you speak French too, Monsieur!" Jessica notes.

"Well, in Montreal, it helps. We relocated here from New Jersey when I was a teenager, and then I had to learn it for business," Paul says, then he adds: "We sometimes speak it at home." He unknowingly gives himself away as being married.

We? She knew it! Jessica opens her mouth to confront Paul about his slip-up and reconsiders. She will learn the truth soon enough. In the meantime, she will have fun and enjoy the ride. *It wasn't as if guys were lining up these days to see her! Not that Paul would ever know!*

"Yes, French is a prerequisite for living here," Jessica retorts evenly, careful not to react. *He could be a single Dad.* Jessica soothes her disappointment.

"Mais oui. Et j'adore le français. C'est tellement romantique!" Paul continues showing off, although he thinks he is displaying his linguistic abilities.

"Oh, you're a romantic, Paul," Jessica coos.

Paul smiles at his ability to turn on the charm as quickly as he turns the key in the ignition. His luxury sports car roars to life. Jessica remembers her morning struggle and makes a mental note to call for a service appointment Monday morning.

"My family hailed from France and settled in Quebec City. "My mother is French-speaking. She is also fluent in English and Spanish. She works as an international interpreter. Dad wanted to learn Spanish to travel with Mom. He retired this winter at fifty-four," Jessica readily shares about her family.

"But your mom still works?" Paul asks.

"Oh yes! Mom is a consummate professional. She's fifty-five." Jessica says.

Paul considers the mid-fifties close to his forty-eight years: *What would Jessica think of his age?*

They head over the Champlain Bridge. Jessica wonders why they are leaving the city when Montreal has countless choice eateries. "Where to, Paul?" she asks.

"Oh, I thought we might go to a quiet little restaurant on the South Shore. But first, I must swing by my office to pick up my paperwork and change. It's on the way," he says.

"You work from home on weekends?" Jessica queries. She guards her weekends.

"Not if I can help it," Paul adds, "but they expect me to have the files handy. The older guys sometimes call Saturdays between rounds on the golf course. Sundays are sacred."

Jessica feels comfortable with this man. She studies his profile as he drives, how his hands deftly control the wheel, and his eyes never stray from the road ahead, noticing that Paul still manages to give the impression he is listening.

"Any music preference?" Paul presses the compact disk player button, realizing Bella's kiddie CD was the last music played. He takes his girls out for breakfast Sunday mornings, letting Irini sleep in at least one day of the week. Bella always insists on choosing the tunes. The older girls tolerate her songs and usually clap and sing in the backseat—*Stop, Paul! Why is he thinking about his children right now?* Paul muses that they typically talk about their children whenever he and Irini go out for a date night. *Is this his default? Or is it merely guilt?*

"I like all kinds of music," Jessica offers. "*Skinnamarinky Dinky Dink* is my favourite," she winks, recognizing the childhood classic Sharon, Lois, and Bram tune wafting from the stereo. *I'm betraying my age*, she muses.

"Yeah, this song is the perfect motivation for sales pitches!" Paul shoots back.

"Do you have any blues?" Jessica asks, sobering at the thought of what it means that Paul has this children's CD on auto-play.

"Blues are coming up," Paul is calm. *Like any self-respecting man looking to get laid listens to children's songs.* He muses, reaches into the compartment between the seats, and finds and replaces the CD. Paul is relieved when blues music plays.

The car fills with melodic sounds, and he pulls into the parking lot of a substantial glass building on Nun's Island. "I'll leave the stereo on. You relax while I whip up to the office," Paul hopes the guys have gone home by now. They tend to leave by three on Fridays. It was the end of a demanding week.

Paul is careful to park away from his colleagues. He knows the tinted windows will keep Jessica a shadow. She resembles Irini from the side—same fair features.

Paul hurries into his office with cursory glances

from the staff, thinning out as he had expected. "Any calls?" he queries Marianne, his loyal secretary, who never asks questions and is eager to please.

"Your wife," Marianne efficiently delivers Paul's messages.

"Thank you. I am not here, okay? I'm just back to retrieve the files I need to work from home this weekend," Paul tells her.

"Understood," Marianne obliges.

Marianne returns to preparing for her weekend as Paul closes his door. He opens his sports bag and retrieves his neat, rolled-up clothes. Paul dresses quickly and calls Irini on his office phone, glancing out the sidelight window and waving to a now departing Marianne. *No one to screen his calls or say whether he is here.* Irini knows Paul never answers after hours to avoid unwanted calls from job searchers and telemarketers.

"Hiya!" an enthusiastic smile in her voice as Irini answers on the fifth ring. She's out of breath.

"Hello, Irini! Catching you running, am I?" Paul's smooth voice doesn't belie any tension or nervousness.

"Oh, I was about to take the kids to swim at Cap-Saint-Jacques. I ran back into the house for Bella's floaties. Are you coming home early today? The kids are happy to have this ped day. Can you join us?" Irini is hopeful.

"That is nice—a trip to the beach," Paul momentarily feels caught between his wife's reasonable request and the act he is about to commit. But he knows hands-down which one he prefers.

"Yes, they have cabin fever. We all do. It will do us good. Meetings finished earlier than expected?" Irini presses. She doesn't feel like writing anymore today; the afternoon sunshine beckons her. She decided this unseasonably hot spring weather is perfect for dipping their toes in the water.

"No. Meetings are going later than expected with the Kessler account. I will be quite late, Honey. Don't wait up for me." As an afterthought, Paul adds, "I have to go over some details the seniors missed. You know, with the company."

"Ah, what will you do for supper? Want me to keep your plate warm?" Irini offers.

"Nah, thanks, Love. I'll grab something fast. It should be a late night," Paul covers his tracks.

"Okay. See you tomorrow. Remember, we promised Bella we would go shopping for her bike. She reminded me again today that she is turning four." Irini doesn't want to disappoint the child.

"Yes, I remember. We can still do that. Give the girls hugs for me, will you?" Paul pulls the phone away from his ear, signalling impatience: "Bye, Irini!"

"Bye, Paul," the phone clicks.

He is free!

Airtight alibi. Irini won't call back this evening. Paul is confident. He cannot feel remorse for the act he is about to commit, let alone the string of other infidelities. Paul reminds himself that these affairs are meaningless, distracting him from his monotonous routine. If Paul were inclined to dig deeper, he'd realize the presence of an unfillable void temporarily quenched by his next conquest.

Paul gathers his paperwork and duffle bag and sprints out of the office to a waiting elevator. No one is around to interrupt his exit. *Perfect.*

The door closes, enveloping Paul in the protective dull piped muzak he hates as his descent begins.

Eight

Jessica and Paul

"Okay, Jess, what do you feel like eating?" Jessica notes that Paul takes license calling her by her shortened name. Now she likes the familiarity.

"I thought you had the restaurant all picked out," Jessica hates deciding where to eat. She and Cassie take forever to choose an eatery. They once commiserated about women's tendency to be too collaborative; even the most straightforward choices are tough because neither wants to make the wrong one! Two professionals making critical decisions cannot decide where to eat! Usually, Cassie withdraws a restaurant card from her purse, somewhere one of her wealthy suitors had taken her the week before. And Cassie often insists on paying with a shiny gold card: "Company perk," she tells Jessica. Jessica is never disappointed in the food and the atmosphere. However, she fantasizes about her best friend huddled at a quiet corner table, her stockinged foot brushing her companion's leg—she is daring and suggestive.

Jessica knows that Cassie loves to be loved by men as she holds the affections of multiple suitors; the constant ringing of her best friend's cell phone means her next date is one call away. But Jessica appreciates her time with Cassie.

Fate brought Jessica and Cassie together during a marketing course in Cassie's short-lived university career when they became fast friends and besties. Brief because of the scandal that broke out after Cassie slept with her *Ethics* professor. When rumours started circulating, he asked her to withdraw from his course. Two months later, Cassie left her studies: "To hell with university—I'm done here!" She cited a family emergency that required she temporarily move to another province. Only Cassie knew the truth behind her absence from Montreal, Jessica, and her life. She needed to deal with an unwanted pregnancy. Cassie had decided she'd buckle down and focus solely on her studies; she had stopped taking the pill so she wouldn't feel tempted to have sex. That backfired! Her doctor found a couple who desperately wanted to adopt her son. *No strings.* Cassie told herself. She wanted a closed adoption.

Jessica went from seeing her best friend every other day and sharing girl talk about campus life to hearing from Cassie once a month when she called to gush about her latest fling with a worldly person: "He is way sexier than that balding *Ethics* prof!" Cassie would giggle. Jessica marvelled at how easily her friend rebounded. She wondered how someone could be cavalier about leaving university studies prematurely when she was concerned about building a career.

Cassie was thriving in her career beyond what Jessica could imagine; she had allegedly worked her way up in sales. Cassie returned to Montreal, and the two women bonded again as though they had never been apart. She attended Jessica's graduation ceremony. Cassie managed to snag a seat near the front, causing a commotion as her late arrival displaced an entire row of people. Dressed in a short red miniskirt, a tight white blouse, and wearing red stilettos, Cassie excused herself as everyone stood to let her pass. This debacle drew the attention of her former lover, the *Ethics* professor sitting on stage, with whom she made eye contact. Cassie grinned and blew him a kiss.

"Are you considering what you want to eat?" Paul interrupts Jessica's reverie.

"Uhm, you choose. I trust you have good taste in restaurants," Jessica accedes.

"Ah, your confidence in me is inspiring," Paul flatters her again. We will go to…." He steers into a restaurant parking lot on a busy strip near the Champlain

Bridge, "this one, Jessica. You will love it." Paul glides into a parking spot and cuts the engine.

Paul leads Jessica from the car into the cozy interior of a quaint Italian restaurant, asking the waiter for a quiet booth in the back. Jessica likes how Paul wants her all to himself. *Or is he trying to hide? And from who—his wife?* Jessica wonders why she feels cautious. She, too, has a plan. Jessica berates herself. *This outing is just a date and not necessarily a prelude to an intimate relationship.* However, Jessica knows that she holds the power to decide the outcome.

She feels excited that today is Friday, the start of the weekend! She will sleep late tomorrow and spend a leisurely afternoon at the spa. Jessica considers herself a spa diva, relishing the various treatments that make her feel pampered and feminine—something no man can do for her. Jessica feels herself letting loose after a bottle of Sangiovese and conversation laced with innuendo.

"So, tell me what you really do in your spare time," Paul probes to understand Jessica's inner world better.

"Besides dreaming of ways to make Kessler more competitive?" Jessica smirks.

"Besides that, Jess. I'm sure you have a full life of your own," Paul's eyes twinkle. He wants to know more about this woman who is as captivating as attractive. *He wants to know her.*

"I hike, ski, socialize, and love a good romance,"

Jessica shares. "And you?" Jessica tries hard to be interested in hearing about this family man, although she'd rather not know the truth.

"I work a lot," Paul uses his job to hide his mundane suburban life.

"All work and no play, as they say," Jessica winks.

"Oh, I play," Paul affirms.

Jessica does not doubt that this self-assured man makes time for fun. This talk is leading somewhere—and Jessica plans to exploit it.

Dessert comes far too soon. Jessica decides to share the mocha mousse delight with Paul and requests two spoons. They savour the creamy chocolate in the glow of the candle. Flushed from the red wine, they lean into one another for a kiss when their utensils touch. Jessica relishes that too: the sweet taste on their tongues circling. *Oh, this French kiss is as decadent as the desert!* Jessica feels a tingling permeate her pelvis.

"Mmm," Paul murmurs into Jessica's lush lips. He is putty in this beautiful woman's hands. The stirring in his loins makes Paul feel alive and virile, arising from dormant feelings that catch him by surprise.

"Shall we go?" Jessica murmurs. She's in control.

"Yes. I have an idea," Paul whispers and pays the tab. He feels excited as he helps Jessica into a spring coat that hugs her curves, touching her waist, then drops his hand to let her attach the belt.

Once again, Paul and Jessica are on the road, wending their way through Friday night traffic, returning to the city, and driving up Mount Royal to see the sights and shining lights. Paul feels giddy: *Who knows where the night will lead?*

Nine

Irini and Paul

Having bathed and put Bella to bed, then tucked in her older girls, Irini settles down to a cup of ginger tea and her writing. She pops a compact disc into the CD player. Irini feels inspired hearing Extreme's Gary Cherone and Nuno Bettencourt's poignant song, *More Than Words*, which topped the 1991 Billboard Hot 100 charts. Irini feels awe when the artists' melodic voices caress the ballad's refrain, echoing her experience as she pieces her legacy together from memories long stashed away. She writes the latest trajectory of thoughts running through her mind, reflecting on how she first met Paul:

Paul was sitting with friends at the university campus café, and Irini could hear their collective intake of breath as she sailed in to grab a coffee between classes.

She had tended to a sick Cassandra all night, and her energy was flagging. *A dose of java might help,* Irini told herself.

"Pssst!" a male voice beckoned.

Irini turned her head toward the testosterone group, hoping the catcall was not a cue for her. She was new here; she didn't have time for friends with her studies and chaotic home life. How could she bring someone to her home, where her mother lay snoring on the sofa, zoned out on pills?

The testosterone-filled table was studying their books like they were cramming for an exam—except for one whose gaze was looking right at Irini, studying *her.* And now he said, "Yes, you!"

Irini blushed. What might he want with her? She felt dishevelled and nondescript. She kept a low profile.

"You dropped your scarf, Lady," the piercing blue mischievous eyes twinkled at her.

Irini didn't see her pink scarf anywhere on the floor, but it wasn't hanging around her neck.

"It will cost you to get it back," he said, running the scarf through his hands. A round of snickers erupted from the testosterone, distracted from their books.

"Oh?" Irini retorted; she had no time for this charade.

"Yes, I am estimating the price," came his sultry reply. He fingered the silky fabric in a gesture that made Irini pause.

"In that case, you can keep it. I am sure pink will go well with that navy jacket of yours," Irini turned to the counter to order the most oversized format of coffee they sold.

More snickers filled the air, and Paul refused to back down: "Bet it would, but pink is not my colour." He was undaunted by her jab.

Irini felt impatient but compelled to respond: "Maybe your girlfriend might like it," she said over her shoulder as she paid the counter server. Then she walked away, carefully holding the hot brew.

Irini heard the collective intake of breath from the group as they stifled their laughter.

He was at her back now, draping the soft scarf around her shoulders: "It looks beautiful on you." He persevered: "It might look even better without anything else."

"What, no girlfriend?" Irini raised a contoured eyebrow. She was annoyed by this guy's bravado.

"No. Want to be one?" he persisted.

Ha! one! She knew it: men like him—making a show of trying to pick her up in front of his friends. "One? As part of a stable, you mean?" Irini shot back, tossing her blonde hair over her shoulder.

"No, one as in you! What are you doing for the rest of your life?" he was poker-faced and undaunted.

"Haven't thought that far ahead, but if you give me

a couple of years, I'll have a business plan all mapped out for you," Irini decided to go for the jugular.

"Come on. Could you go easy on me? I want to take you out," he was perseverant: "What is your name?"

Irini relented as a smile cracked her lips; she relaxed, the tension in her body giving way to *What if?*

"Irini Caliani," she offered her manicured hand to shake his well-groomed one.

He extended his massive grip and said: "Want to get out of here?"

"I am getting out of here. I have a class in five minutes. Next time," Irini turned to leave. His eyes bore into her, and his homies' jeers followed her out of the café. She felt a gentle tugging on her arm.

"Wait! You didn't say when!" It was him again! The guy was relentless! He followed Irini to the elevator that would whisk her away from the discomfort of this unasked-for attention.

"When," Irini's mind already visualizing the assignment she had worked into the late hours of the night to finish; it was due upon entering class. "And you didn't tell me your name," she shot back.

"My name is Paul Caldwell," Paul persevered, his sparkling eyes melting Irini's resolve, "When can we see each other again?"

"I may be free this weekend. Let me check my schedule," Irini's reply was sombre.

"Right. Then give me your number," Paul insisted,

pulling out what looked like the syllabus for a business course and turning it over on top of his binder.

Irini hesitated: *What if her doped-up mother answers the phone? What if her much younger sister, Cassandra, takes the call and forgets to give Irini the message? What if Paul doesn't call anyway? He might never look at his syllabus. These guys chase women instead of consulting their course outlines for the next assignment due date.*

"Your number. Do you have a telephone?" Paul's voice cut into Irini's worries.

"Here," Irini scribbled the phone number on Paul's course outline and shoved it into his hands, expecting he would never follow through. *Guys like him have tons of girls running after them. Why choose her?*

"Call you tonight then!" And with that, Paul strode back to his friends, and Irini caught the open elevator, grateful she still had two minutes before class started. She felt lighter and less panicked about handing in her assignment as her mind replayed the scenario with Paul Caldwell. Irini walked into class smiling.

◆ ◆ ◆

That evening, despite her better judgment, Irini hovered near the phone after making the meal, clearing the dishes, and checking that her siblings had finished their homework. Their mother dozed on the sofa amidst the chaos of a house busy preparing for the next day:

Lena made the lunches while Irini coaxed Gianni into the shower.

"Done," Gianni, a typical boy, emerged after less than five minutes. "Can I watch TV now?" he asked.

"Yes, but low volume, so you don't wake Ma," Irini cautioned him.

Irini bathed Cassandra, towel-dried her brown locks, and put her to bed at seven, relishing the time to prepare her assignments for the coming week. Then the phone rang. And it was Paul! True to his word, he was calling—her! She walked from the kitchen to her bedroom next door with the long cord to avoid disturbing her sleeping mother.

"What? Who's that? Your father? Tell him to fuck off! The bastard never calls to say he'll be late!" Irini's mother fell back into her drug-induced nap on the sofa despite the television's low hum and flickering images.

Irini covered the phone receiver as she told Paul, "One moment, please," and called out, "It's for me, Ma!" She retreated to her room, closed the door, and moved to her bed, where she would languish over the first of countless long telephone conversations with Paul.

"Sounds like your mom doesn't approve of male suitors," Paul chuckled.

"No, no, nothing like that! She thought it was my father. He's like a cat; he rarely comes home." *Why was she disclosing herself to Paul? It was too soon to share family tales,* Irini reminded herself.

"Ah, that must be tough," Paul consoled into the phone.

Irini softened: "It's how things are," Irini brushed off the opportunity to elaborate further.

"How was your class today?" Paul was curious about Irini. He wanted to know more about this woman who had rebuffed him in front of his friends.

Irini was happy to change the subject and wondered if Paul was diplomatic or didn't care. *And why did she want him to, anyway?* Irini reminded herself that the less said about her home life, the better to avoid scaring Paul away. "Good, thanks. We had to hand in a paper first thing."

"What kind of course has you writing papers?" Paul queried. Paul's courses gave multiple choice exams and case studies. He was grateful for his study group—primarily girls who fawned over him and were extremely happy to take on the load.

Her mother never asked what program Irini was studying, so she liked that Paul was interested. "Child development. I am doing a double major in English literature and psychology," Irini explained.

"Have you figured me out yet?" Paul asked.

Irini thought Paul was pretentious: "Yes, you are still a child in development!" she teased.

"Good one! And yes, I am!" Paul quipped. "And

you're quick on the draw, Irini!" She could feel her face flush. Her life at home had prepared her to deliver careful, quick comebacks. It was part of the dysfunction, watching her father drink and her mother wilt away on drugs while Irini rescued and covered up to maintain a sense of normalcy in her abysmal home life.

Theirs was the start of a cautious but whirlwind courtship. Irini intrigued Paul: he viewed her as an exquisite, self-determined creature he could love and protect. Paul stole Irini's heart; there was no doubt in her mind that he was 'The One.' Although Paul was graduating, she wanted to complete her studies as she was in her second semester. He would work and establish his career while Irini finished university.

Irini worried about her two youngest siblings she would leave in her mother's harried care, but her life was taking shape, and she would not look back. Irini did not want to be a case study in her social psychology text: a spinster with no time or energy to build her own life because she was stuck raising her siblings. Besides, she craved the chance to create a close couple that would nurture their children, unlike Irini's jaded parents. While Irini knew that guys mostly wanted to score, she was seeking someone who would love and protect her—she hoped that Paul Caldwell could be that someone.

Ten

Jessica and Cassie

"What do you mean; you *think* he may be married?" Cassie probes Jessica while swirling ice cubes around her dirty vodka martini. They are sitting in a quiet corner of another undiscovered gem of a restaurant that Cassie has introduced to Jessica.

"He doesn't wear a ring. I swear I saw one when he came with his team for our PR pitch," Jessica's brow furrows; she tries to remember and visualize what she saw or did not see. How could she have imagined it? How could she not have noticed when she remarked so much about the man—from his poise to how he flicked his too-long sandy-blond hair away from his penetrating blue eyes?

"Many married men don't wear their rings. Did you ask him?" Cassie presses.

"I called him out on it. And he told me no. I didn't press," Jessica feels backed into a corner.

"Well, didn't you come right out and ask, 'Are you married?'" Cassie insists.

"Why? That would only show interest. And anyway, it's so cliché," Jessica tosses her strawberry blonde tresses. She is wearing an off-the-shoulder top with sequins that catch the low light above their table, making her face radiant.

"How many times have you seen him?" Cassie asks.

"Just once—yesterday evening. We have plans again tomorrow," Jessica shrugs. She knows this thing with Paul is casual.

"He doesn't sound married to me!" Cassie scoffs, considering the men she dates. They get away one night a week, usually when the pressure builds to the point where they need a sexual release.

Jessica is still not convinced. "He made a handful of slips. He had a children's music CD in his car stereo—another tip-off! He quickly changed it." Jessica knew men who had shared custody of their children. *Paul probably has kids with an ex.*

"So what? No strings, Jess! Who wants marriage anyway? Let her have him!" Cassie sermonizes Jessica, "She can wash his socks and wipe his kids' noses. You get the good stuff. You get to make it *good* for him after all that domesticity." Cassie explains her approach to the men she sees. *She offers the best of herself, which they enjoy. And in return, they take care of her expenses and rent. Plus, her lifestyle affords her luxuries like spas, massages, gym trainers, designer wear, and trendy restaurants.*

"Yes. But Cassie, it's tiring having to try so hard. Sometimes I want what my friends have: stability, knowing, and yes, a guarantee," Jessica insists.

"Ah yes, wedded bliss," Cassie sounds bitter.

Jessica admits to her friend and herself for the first time: "I'm fed up with the meat market and the dating scene." Jessica locates her feelings of loneliness.

"That's the problem with women when they land the guy, Jess. They stop making up, and they put up. They go from lithe sex kittens with unique interests and exciting lives to frump. You want that?" Cassie is smug; she paints a dim portrait of married life and sits back in her seat, sipping the remnants of her diluted cocktail through a tiny stir straw.

"No, I guess not—not that part of it. But I do want children. And you need stability for that," Jessica sighs.

Cassie considers Jessica's last sentence, contemplating her own failure at motherhood. She knows she doesn't have a maternal bone in her body and cannot support Jessica's desire to mother a child and do the domestic scene. Cassie had never shared the story of Isabella with Jessica or any of her other unwanted pregnancies. It felt like something she needed to keep private. Cassie felt shame and worried her friend would judge her, so she also hadn't shared with Jessica what marketing her 'job' entails. *She'd never understand.* But Cassie knows that maternal instinct is a driving force for many women. "These are the 1990's, Jessica. You can have a child by yourself," she tries to be helpful.

"I suppose…" Jessica grows pensive, "that is if I can even have children. When I went for my pap test yesterday, my doctor told me I have a tilted uterus. So, it might be difficult getting pregnant." Jessica recalls how her gynecologist probed around the inside while pressing on her belly. It had sent shock waves through her body. She could fathom the pain of childbirth.

"Well, the decision might be made for you then," Cassie concludes, her comment striking Jessica as uncompassionate. Jessica had noticed Cassie's lack of maternal instincts, but tonight she wondered if her best friend had any empathy.

"Anyway, raising a kid without a partner is a lonely road. I would want my child to have both parents involved. It must be so much work for one parent, and from my understanding, it's mainly the mother," Jessica concludes with certainty. She is eager to change the subject to one with more common ground.

"Yeah, must be. But many mothers are single parents, even inside their couples," Cassie averts her gaze. Staring into her empty martini glass, Cassie says: "Well, time to order another drink or go home."

"I'm ready," Jessica gathers her handbag and coat.

"An early night—okay, let's go," Cassie agrees. "In

the meantime, consider asking the guy if he is married—put your mind at ease. You know, they never leave their wives. What did you say his name is?"

"Oh, I didn't! It's Pa—" Jessica's words fade into the restaurant din as Cassie turns to greet an older handsome red-haired man passing their table.

"Regan, nice to see you again!" she gushes, touching his arm.

"Cass, long time, I'd say! How are you?" he folds Cassie into an embrace that strikes Jessica as too long and tight.

"Wonderful, Regan. And you?" Cassie buries her head into Regan's neck. He is tall and lean.

Regan pulls back, still holding Cassie's toned arms, "Fine. Fine. Hey, are you leaving now? Do you have time to catch up over a quick drink?" Regan does not notice Jessica standing beside her friend, feeling awkward.

"Yes, but surely you are not here alone, Regan?" Cassie is oblivious to Jessica.

"I am. I came from another late Saturday at the office. This place serves the best burgers. You know how it goes: you miss dinner, and the pickings are slim. I thought I would forage here rather than in the fridge," Regan shrugs.

"Ah, wifey doesn't do leftovers?" Cassie asks.

"Nah, the kids are all gone. What's the point?" Regan smiles "Besides, seeing you here makes the thought of that burger all the tastier! Do stay!" he winks.

"Alright. Jess, will you excuse me? Let's talk tomorrow," Cassie waves Jessica off in favour of her male companion.

Jessica hugs her friend: "Certainly, but not tomorrow. I have a date, remember? Night, Cassie!" She turns to Regan: "Nice to meet you, Regan." Jessica sends a dig to Cassie about her abrupt change of plan and hurries out of the restaurant. She envies her friend's confidence with men.

"Bye-bye, Jessica!" Cassie calls through her laughter, settling into the seat Jessica had vacated, and Regan slips in next to her.

Jessica catches a glimpse of the cuddling couple as she exits into the chilly night and wonders how her friend does it. She observes Cassie's never-ending potential for a date unfold on weekends and most weeknights. She wonders how her friend keeps late hours and still manages to work the following day. Then again, tomorrow is Sunday. Jessica relishes the thought of sleeping in and preparing for a delicious afternoon with Paul.

Eleven

Paul, Irini, and Bella

"We promised her, Paul," Irini reminds her husband about their planned trip to the bicycle shop with Bella this Saturday afternoon when he comes out of the shower after sleeping late. She cannot blame him—Paul had burned the midnight oil last night—Irini considers that Paul must feel exhausted from working on a massive project.

"I know, and I still want to buy her the bike, but shouldn't we check with Cassandra first? I mean, Bella *is* her daughter," Paul protests, hedging—he's trying to bide his time. *He'd love to lounge around today and fantasize about seeing Jess tomorrow!*

Four years later, they still had not completed the legal wrangling, granting full custody of Isabella to Paul and Irini. Cassandra had approached her brother,

Gianni, a family lawyer, the logical person to complete the adoption. But he kept pushing it off: "I'll get to it. She's still with Irini, so what's the hurry?"

When Bella turned two in 1989, Irini had become impatient, telling Paul: "It's high time we finalize this!" She would call Gianni herself.

Paul shrugged: "Irini, it makes no difference to our arrangement. Cassandra told you she considers us Bella's parents.

Gianni had been evasive like he didn't want to do the paperwork. "We expect to pay your fee, Gianni," Irini had said.

"You're family, Irini, so no need. I'll file with the court as soon as my research is complete," he assured her.

Irini had wondered: *What research? Cassandra could easily say who the father is—if she wanted to.* "I think she knows who the father is—speak to her, Gian," Irini suggested. She never heard back from Gianni. No one followed up or forced the issue, and eventually, the matter fell into the abyss of busy family life. It was working fine; 'Don't fix it if it isn't broken' appeared to be the motto.

"Paul, that's ridiculous! Cassandra has given us parental authority on greater decisions than this!" Irini is impatient. She looked forward to seeing the smile on Bella's face when they gave her the purple bicycle she had requested for her birthday. She can picture handlebars with streamers flying in the wind as she shadows the little girl on the sidewalk of their quiet street. Irini feels that Bella will be safe with training wheels and a helmet.

"Then call Cassandra, please. Ask if she's okay with it," Paul pleads. He knows better from co-parenting with Irini than making decisions without the mother's input.

"Fine," Irini storms off to search for the wireless phone one of the older girls had mislaid.

Moments later, Paul hears Irini on the phone with Cassandra and realizes by their laughter that it will be a while. He settles on the sofa with the Saturday newspaper; he loses himself in reverie while reading and re-reading the same two lines of an article about a hostile business takeover. Paul reminisces about his evening with Jessica and how he didn't want it to end when he crawled out of her bed and into his sometime during the wee morning hours, a twenty-five-minute drive between the two. Irini was sleeping soundly on her side of their king-size bed with Bella snuggling in the middle. Bella must have felt scared from her nightmare the previous night, and Paul figured that Irini was not taking any chances that she would awaken to another round of horrific screams. No one had stirred as he pulled the sheets and crawled in. He had felt tired but sated.

"She's fine with it, Honey. Let's go!" Irini interrupts Paul's reverie.

"Uh…Oh, great!" Paul stands.

An hour later, they watch their littlest charge marvelling at all the colours in the bicycle shop, repeating, "But I want the one with the strings!" when she doesn't see any models with streamers hanging from the handlebars.

"Love, they are extra. We can add them," Irini soothes.

"But I want them on this bicycle!" Bella pouts, pointing to a purple glimmer painted bicycle with training wheels.

The sales associate leaves them momentarily and returns: "Like these?" She kneels before the little girl, holding pink handlebar grips with long shimmering pink streamers.

"Yes!" Bella's eyes light up as she squeals with delight.

"We can install them for you right now if this is the bike you want," the sales associate calls after her. Bella is already on the bike, riding down the aisle. She calls over her shoulder, "Yes. Now, please!"

Paul and Irini exchange smiles and chuckles as they watch this little girl claim precisely what she wants. They persuade Bella to dismount the bike to try on a matching pink helmet, proving a snug fit around her curls. *She will be safe. She is good to go.*

"No extra charge for the grips," the clerk rings up the bright bicycle and helmet sale.

"Thank you!" Paul pulls a wad of cash out of his pocket, and Irini notices the absence of his wedding ring. She assumes he left it in the shower. She makes a mental note to rescue it later.

Walking to the car, Isabella bobs up and down, asking if she could ride her new bike home. Irini laughs, telling Bella that their house is too far away. Irini reminds her how fresh she will feel after napping, making her first ride more enjoyable.

"No nap! I want to ride today!" Bella insists.

"I'll take you," Paul offers. He wants to please the little girl.

Irini feels relieved, for she is eager to return to her writing sanctuary and flesh out the thoughts that had been pulling at her lately. She cannot help herself: "Your ring, Paul?"

"Oh, it is in my gym bag from my workout yesterday," he half-lies.

"The one you also didn't have time for when we asked you to join us at the lake. Something about meetings all day," Irini presses, stopping at their vehicle and looking Paul in the eye.

"It was short," Paul's reply is just as brief.

"Ah," Irini feels guilty. *I make time for my workouts—how can I begrudge Paul his?*

Paul busies himself loading the bike into the back of their SUV, happy for a task to hide behind.

Twelve

Irini

Irini snatches two hours to write while Paul has taken the kids out for breakfast this Sunday morning, a ritual he observes, letting her sleep in. No lie-in today—Irini's brain is swirling with a flood of new memories. She wants to empty her mind before the week starts, and the routine usurps her creativity:

Irini's mother, Katerina Kaminski, was a Polish immigrant who had suffered the horrors of the Holocaust. Katerina was a survivor. She married Gino mere months after he first laid eyes on her as she hovered between a hollowed-out structure and a pile of rubble, sheltering from the shelling around her.

"Are you alone?" Gino had asked Katerina. He kept his gaze level with hers, looking into her limpid eyes to avoid staring at her feminine curves, apparent in her tattered underwear. She was beautiful, in contrast to the wreckage around her.

Katerina flinched, recalling Tata's earlier words about the enemy.

Gino's heart lurched, watching her tremble, and it hurt him to witness the war's atrocities: levelled homes, orphaned children, and dismembered soldiers. Gino counted his blessings that he was alive. This scene haunted him; the sudden eerie quiet around them was a reprieve that called him to act. Gino did not want to spook the girl, but she needed to leave. And he wanted to bring her to safety.

Katerina nodded, her emerald-green eyes anchored on his. The fear in those eyes was more than he could bear.

Gino tapped his chest: "Gino," to signal his name and give the frightened teen some comfort in his gesture.

"Katerina," she tapped back, feeling more at ease with this soldier. He had a kind, gentle face despite the stubble lining his jaw.

Gino wrapped the shivering Katerina in an emergency blanket from his kit and coaxed her forward before the low building crumbled. She let him put a protective arm around her shoulder to guide her to his armoured vehicle.

Gino put Katerina up in a safe house in Poland, where she stayed for one month, regaining her strength.

Gino would check on her when he could. Despite the language barrier, bolstered by what little English they mustered, their bond was immediate and forged out of their individual need for each other and stability during wartime. Gino and Katerina married in a brief ceremony where a Polish court blessed them three months later. As the war ended in 1945, they joined Gino's family in Canada, seeking safety and a peaceful new life.

The newlywed pair's first-born daughter in 1946 was a surprise to the family. A healthy baby girl who barely cried had a temperament that bore no resemblance to the violence in which she was conceived. They named her Irini, derived from Katerina, the namesake declaring that the child belonged to her mother, not to the rogue who had stolen Katerina's virginity during a war that stripped her home, family, and dignity. If not for the Caliani name, Irini would have been an illegitimate child.

Gino assured Katerina that this child was just as much his: "I love you, and this baby comes from you, so I love her, too!"

If only Katerina had the same maternal feelings. When she breastfed Irini, Katerina saw the violent soldier pulling at her tender nipple while thrusting into her. She was appalled at how this act of feeding her daughter caused a visceral reaction. So, when Irini cried and failed to feed properly, and the doctor suggested her milk was no good, to switch to infant formula, Katerina felt relieved. When Irini's middle-of-the-night wailing would go unanswered, Gino got up to feed the baby.

A sob catches in Irini's throat; she feels wracked with the heartache about how she was conceived—a cellular reaction imprinted in her core. She believes this brutal fact of her grim beginnings in life has far-ranging effects on her body. A naturopath she often sees for reconnective healing work had suggested to Irini that childhood grief lay dormant in her body, later expressing itself as fibromyalgia. *How can the mind harbour a secret that the body knows from an early consciousness?* Irini had rejected this sentiment as woo-woo; now, she sees it in a new light: *We internalize and integrate the things that fragment us.*

Despite Katerina's underlying hatred of Irini, the girl basked in childhood naiveté. Gino cherished his beloved Irini; he didn't display any different attitude toward the child sired from a seed that was not his own. Gino's love for Irini was equal to his passion for words. He would spend hours reading to the little girl. Holding the child in his lap, Gino enjoyed opening the oversized sheets of the daily newspaper, wrapping them around Irini like a protective cocoon as he read her stories and current events. He taught her to write before she started school; he asked her to pen letters to him about her day. Writing helped Irini cope with the escalating wrath of her mother.

Katerina had told four-year-old Irini that she was special and how an angel had planted her in the woman's womb amid the chaos of the war. But Katerina mostly ignored Irini as she grew, grateful that the child could keep herself entertained with books and writing in her diary. Then Katerina turned, unleashing long-held resentment toward her daughter: "You're the devil's spawn!" she had spewed one day while Irini, now seven years old, was too young to comprehend.

"Daddy, what does spawn mean?" Irini had asked Gino that evening as they read together.

"It means to birth something or someone—a child. That's a big word for a little one. Where did you learn that?" Gino chuckled.

His laughter turned to fury when she replied: "Ma says I'm the devil's spawn."

Later Irini could hear her parents bickering through the paper-thin walls: "What kind of mother says that to her child?" Gino shouted. Shockwaves reverberated when he slammed the front door as he left the house. He didn't return until late the next day, the start of a common occurrence as he would leave the house for long stretches.

Irini felt isolated and responsible for driving her father away: *It's all my fault.*

Katerina blamed her deteriorating relationship with Gino on Irini. In her frustration, she tipped her hand to Mamma Caliani, hoping they would side with her against Gino. The senior Caliani's questioned whether the circumstances of Irini's illegitimacy had forced Gino into marriage. They took their ire out on Katerina, who, in turn, treated Irini like an interloper.

In 1958 a vengeful recession took hold, and Gino drifted from job to job. Irini felt like Cinderella at twelve years old as she took on more responsibilities when their family spiralled further into a pit of despair and began to collapse. Life had been abundant and jolly when Gino worked, but with each job loss, he joined the unemployment line, his self-esteem plummeted, and they lived scarcity.

Despite his doting, it was also around this time that Gino stopped sharing his love of reading with Irini. She was old enough to fetch her books from the local library. Fortunately, they still bonded over talking about the books she read. That is when Gino was home or sober enough to pay attention. He tried: "Tell me what you're reading. You are reading something, eh?" Gino always wanted to ensure that Irini kept up her library card, which was free. The recession couldn't take that away from her.

Irini's younger sister, ten-year-old Lena, jealous of her father's bond with 'this half-sister,' broke the bubble one day after spending a weekend with the Caliani grandparents. Their relationship with Gino had been on the rocks because Gino's drinking had worsened, making him unreliable—he'd tell them he'd visit and would not show up or arrive late and drunken. Mamma Caliani blamed Katerina for trapping her Gino into marriage and labelled Irini 'that bastard child,' exposing the circumstances of her birth to Lena.

Lena gloated with this new knowledge and began her onslaught of cruel tricks on Irini. She found and cut out all the pictures of Irini in her family photo booklet. Katerina's acrimony compounded Lena's treatment of Irini, and Irini started to internalize the pain of her reality. The family's relationship with Gino's parents finally succumbed because of their treacherous gossip to Lena. Irini wondered how cruel these grandparents were to tell a child such intimate and horrid detail.

Irini knew she was an outcast and a disgrace to the Caliani name. And Katerina encouraged Lena's taunts that caused so much sibling rivalry. She blamed Irini instead of chastising Lena and mediating to restore peace: "You must learn to be nicer to your sister," Katerina admonished Irini: "After all, she is younger than you!"

Bolstered by Katerina's approval, Lena's unrelenting malice took on a macabre quality: Irini would find dead bugs and birds on her pillow. When she reported the offences to her mother, Katerina spat: "Serves you right for leaving your bedroom window open!"

Irini could not understand her mother's vengeance and how she protected Lena, no matter how grave the injustice was. As she matured, Irini suspected her mother was jealous of the deep bond Irini shared with her father, and Lena mirrored her mother's resentment.

"He's not even your real father; he loves you more!" Lena had spat at Irini.

Irini had no words to express the empty and guilt-ridden feelings about Lena begrudging her their father's attention. She merely walked away with sadness and wished she'd never been conceived, reminding herself that she was forced upon Katerina. *No wonder she doesn't love me. I am an outsider.*

When her brother Gianni was born, Irini connected with her sibling. He revered his big sister. Gianni's birth was Irini's shining light in the sea of darkness that formed her family dynamics. But it forged another point of despair because Gianni's arrival pushed Lena into the unfortunate status of the middle child. *If only I had not been born, Lena would be the lucky first child and Gianni the baby. The family constellation would work well.* Irini recalled this obsessive mindset that besieged her whole childhood.

Katerina did her best to keep the shattered family together, taking odd sewing jobs and housecleaning stints to feed and clothe them. She never knew if Gino would show up with a paycheck—or the remnants of one—showering gifts upon them to assuage his guilt. Gino always gave Irini the most significant present. He once gifted her a boxed set of her beloved author, C.S. Lewis, and gave the other children comic books. These gifts never amended the searing pain Irini felt, her family's woes resting on the bane of her existence.

Gino's battle with alcohol was raging; he'd frequent the bar after work and return in the wee hours of the morning—when he did come home. Gino would tumble into bed beside Katerina, his pungent breath awakening her if she weren't already sleeping fitfully, worrying over his whereabouts. She'd medicate her insomnia with sleeping pills and eventually began using the living room sofa as her bed—all day.

The kids at school teased Irini and called her dad 'Gin the drunk,' repeating what their parents gossiped to other neighbours. Irini swallowed these bitter words the way her adoptive father gulped down gin. She never had the heart to tell her beloved dad about these hurtful rumours.

An ironic twist of fate brought baby Cassandra into the Caliani clan. Born in 1960—six years after Gianni—she resulted from Gino's infidelity with a prostitute. He took the tiny bundle home to Katerina, who already struggled to raise three energetic children while her absentee husband flitted from bar to bar. Katerina felt broken by despair: a mix of guilt, shame, and resentment. She blamed Irini and deep down, herself for being raped: *No wonder Gino runs around—I am the mother of someone else's child. Gino has taken pity on me.* Still, she cursed him for his infidelity and betrayal.

Although she felt obligated to welcome this

stray child and care for it as Gino had done for Irini, Katerina's spirit was too broken to tend to her children, let alone this new baby. The three siblings would eventually pick up the pieces of Gino's and Katerina's inability to deal with their respective grief.

Irini took Cassandra under her wing. By then, Irini was fourteen, and this new baby distracted her from Lena's and her mean-girl friends' onslaught: "You can babysit Cassandra—she's a mutt just like you!" twelve-year-old Lena taunted.

Moving from her scattered thoughts about the crushing dynamics of her family, Irini ponders each character's trajectory and where she and her siblings are now. Their parents died within two years of each other. During winter 1980, Gino was found slumped over the bar while sitting on his favourite barstool; he'd died from alcohol poisoning. Her mother died in the spring of 1982 while dozing on the sofa—from a heart attack: *Poor Mom died of a broken heart.*

Lena forged a life as a minister's wife where she basks in her morality. Irini scoffs: *How fitting for someone who ran a terror campaign against me growing up!* Lena doesn't speak to any of them except Gianni; she'd stopped responding to Irini's messages years ago. Although it is a pain point for Irini, she had let it go, deciding that a relationship with Lena would only spell misery.

Married and with two children, Gianni's life appears

idyllic. An accomplished lawyer, Gianni has followed in his father's footsteps; he is a defender of another kind. He had once told Irini: "Not everyone comes from the nice families you write about in your novels. I represent the underdog—people like our parents."

Irini turns her thoughts to Cassandra, her half-sister and symbiotic outcast who deferred to Irini as a mother figure when both were growing up bereft of a maternal role model. Now in her early thirties, Cassandra flits from man to man. Like her biological mother, Cassandra carves a living from prostitution as a high-class escort, capitalizing on disenfranchised married men. She specializes in affluent men who can support her lifestyle and obsession with sex and shopping. With her long legs, feminine curves, and handsome dark features, Cassandra fits the bill for these men whose money buys them fulfilled fantasies without hassle or commitment. Having completed a year of university, Cassandra would make her street-prostitute mother proud, although Isabelle died from HIV/AIDS when Cassandra was four years old.

Irini married Paul right after university, and they waited until their early thirties to have children while Irini developed her reputation as a novelist. She cultivates the normalcy she had never lived in her childhood. Irini's writing career is flexible and complements her schedule as a mother. She authors novels about wholesome, ordinary people, places, and things—people she has never been or connected with and places she has discovered as an adult. She and Paul travelled to exotic foreign lands during their first eight years of marriage. They visited botanical gardens and zoos in Singapore, rode in a Cessna over Angel Falls in Venezuela, soaked in a seaside mud volcano in Arboletes, Colombia, swam in the turquoise waters of The Seychelles Islands, attended Milan Fashion Week, and built an igloo and dogsledded in the Arctic.

Paul comes from an affluent family. He had every luxury growing up in a stately Westmount home overlooking Montreal: nannies, trips abroad, the best private schools and tutors, and parents who believed in him. Mister Caldwell senior owned multiple businesses and brokered company acquisitions and mergers: "You'll make your way in this world and earn your fortune before inheriting ours," Paul's father had repeatedly told him.

Paul is a maverick in business, comfortable embarking on new ventures backed by his family's money and a business degree. He has done well for himself and his family.

Irini considers how she was lucky to meet Paul as a first-year student while he was in his last semester of university. She was even more fortunate that Paul waited for her to graduate two years later when they could marry and plan for their own family. At first, Paul's doting parents showed their lukewarm approval of the idea—they wanted the best for their only son. They grew to love Irini like their own when she made them grandparents.

Irini hears the car pull up; she wanders to the attic window seat and looks down at her children spilling from the vehicle. Bella's chocolate curls bounce in the sunlight. At four years old, she has her mother's long legs. Bella's got the bluest eyes that Irini thinks she is looking into the ocean's depths.

Peals of laughter ring out. Bella is happy. The way the sunlight touches her face, she resembles the two older girls. *Bella's looks are a trompe l'oeil,* Irini concedes, realizing that people living together often mirror each other and adopt similar mannerisms.

Irini fears Cassandra will one day settle down and find her maternal bent. Irini would feel lost without Bella, having grown to love this toddler as energetic as her mother but more even-tempered and serene. Life in the Caldwell household, with a child-centred focus and routine, is more wholesome for this little girl.

Paul embraces this added child. Irini believes Paul's act of humanity toward Irini's sister makes meaningful amends for Irini's back story. When he arrives home from work, Paul scoops Bella into his lap for a quick story. Bella squeals with delight: "Another one, Poppa!" Irini enjoys watching them bond over story time—and she loves Paul for his gentleness with Bella.

Irini and Paul had braced themselves for these first

labels of "Momma" and "Poppa," not wanting to take anything away from Cassandra. But Cassandra felt no maternal bond with the girl, and they had readily agreed that Irini and Paul would raise Bella as their own. Cassandra would sign papers for Paul and Irini to legalize their arrangement, although this adoption took a back seat to the demands of daily life.

Interesting how history repeats itself. Irini muses as she settles back into writing her memoir. She feels sad about her niece's suspicious origins and wonders if Cassandra ever considered the repetitive hand of fate that Irini has identified. Cassandra has a blind spot regarding her history. Irini cannot expect her readiness to deal with the Caliani family's dysfunction to enter Cassandra's consciousness. *Each sibling interprets their reality differently in their own time*, she concedes.

What would they tell Bella, and will the child learn she was unwanted because of a paid sex deal? These are tough questions directing Irini's writing. Irini wants to believe that Bella is the product of one of Cassandra's more meaningful affairs, and the affluent father does not want his name to appear on the birth certificate, worried it might come back to haunt his marriage. They are usually high-profile men; an illegitimate child would complicate things if the media got wind of it. The writer in Irini always puts a positive fantasy spin on sordid tales—the only way she could cope with her grievous past.

Cassandra had gotten her tubes tied right after giving birth; she could not risk another unwanted pregnancy. However, this time, doctors diagnosed her with hyperemesis gravidarum. This life-threatening constant nausea and vomiting landed a dehydrated and malnourished Cassandra in the hospital—she had never felt so ill! She wondered if all-day morning sickness was her penance for not wanting this baby as soon as the line showed positive on the pregnancy test. Cassandra had tried to talk herself out of it, hiding away from friends and family while deciding what she would do. The first trimester gave way to the second; abortion was no longer a choice. Cassandra would be a mother or find someone to adopt her baby. She chose the latter: making Paul and Irini the adoptive parents had allowed her the best of both worlds.

Irini missed their late-night talks over the phone after taking Bella in. She sensed Cassandra's pain about her mothering Bella. *Or was Cassandra too occupied with the men in her life?* When Bella turned two, Cassandra started visiting bi-weekly and playing the role of doting auntie, to Bella's delight. Although Irini was pleased to watch her sister's blooming relationship with her child, she felt a pang of possessiveness and wondered: *Why now? Is Cassandra's maternal instinct kicking in?* She feared that Cassandra would reconsider.

Irini's head pounds as she triages all the branches of her family tree that provide the fodder for her memoir. Indeed, her family of origin has its redeeming qualities. The ones that stand out are resilience and the need to stay in touch. Holiday gatherings are festive; the house vibrates with the generous laughter of Irini's and Gianni's children. Cassandra lavishes them with toys and chocolate treats.

Their sister, Lena, is absent. She had once told Irini: "My husband's parish has upstanding members who need me." Irini understood upstanding meant that these churchgoing strangers were more worthy of Lena's time and friendship.

Irini combs through the keepsake box on her desk. The vintage hand-painted tin holds the memorabilia Mamma Caliani had kept for her beloved Gino: black-and-white Polaroid photos, writing contest awards, and his poetry. Katerina had added Gino's metal dog tags and The Medal for Military Valour—Medaglia al valor militare—an Italian award for his exceptional courage and initiative on the battlefield. Irini recalls how she'd found a young Gianni fingering Gino's medal and then asking Katerina: "Can I bring this to school for show and tell?"

Gino had kept a diary, which Irini also found when her mother died. She leafs through the faded, penned entries and reads one:

The shelling is all around us. I have been up for twenty-one hours straight. I thought the gin would help, but I'm awake and fuzzy. My comrade died today, and my mind keeps replaying how he fell beside me before we could take cover. I had no time to think—I dragged my other fallen comrade into the trench and stemmed the bleed from his shrapnel wound. They airlifted him out alive.

Then another:

Enemy fire was furious today. I smeared the blood of my fallen comrade on my uniform and had to play dead amongst them, along with one other soldier. When the enemy came to remove our dog tags, mine lay hidden in my front vest pocket. I held my breath. They took my ID from my back pocket. I hope Mamma does not receive word that I'm dead. My comrade was not so fortunate. The enemy saw his breath and shot him directly in the head.

Irini flips to the last page. Gino's final entry is the most poignant:

We ship out tomorrow, and it is not a moment too soon. I am looking forward to reuniting with my beautiful Katerina. We will stay in Warsaw for a week and seek an officiant to marry us. I cannot wait to start my life with her and bring her to

Canada. We will have a home with an enormous vegetable garden and babies, and we will always love each other. One more day, dear Katerina. Please wait for me. I will bring you to freedom.

Tears roll down Irini's cheeks, and her body trembles; she feels overcome by sadness and anger. *How could Katerina doubt Gino's love for her? What made Gino turn to liquor and sex for fulfillment? And why did they both waste this freedom they so desperately wanted?*

Thirteen

Paul and Jessica

"I couldn't wait to see you again," Paul murmurs into Jessica's tousled wet hair. They took a shower together after making love for the second time today. Paul could not remember the last time he'd felt this much libido: like he could go on forever. He marvels at his stamina. He met Jessica two days ago, and already they'd had sex a handful of times!

She lay on her back, caressing her thigh, still glistening with water droplets. *Jessica's orgasms start with a ripple, then come in waves, one after another!* Paul wants to retake her, enter her slowly this time, and bring her to the crests of those pleasure waves, watching her lithe young body shiver and tremble as she comes, not once but multiple times.

He can't help comparing Jessica with Irini, from

whom he must work hard to coax one orgasm. Paul concludes that Irini is preoccupied—she would rather make love to her writing. He doesn't dare let himself stray into guilt. Instead, he hardens, rolls over, and gently pushes himself into Jess' womanhood. They start moving, their rhythm coordinated as though they'd been doing this forever.

Paul looks at his watch; the afternoon has morphed into the evening as the afternoon sun sinks below the skyline. He is too late for Sunday dinner. As if on cue, his cell phone rings. Paul grabs it from the bedside table, fumbles, and presses the ominous green icon. When he replies to her query, Irini can hear the tension in Paul's voice: "Give me another hour, and I'll be home. Keep my dinner warm, please," then he responds to Irini's *I love you*: "I do, too." He hangs up, simple as that. Paul meets Jessica's gaze, and she looks away briefly.

"Your wife," Jessica confirms, disheartened. Jessica had an inkling Paul was married and had not pressed. She did not care because her need supersedes the truth. *I'll take what I can get,* Jessica consoles herself. She is accustomed to men like Paul. They always have somewhere else to be.

"Yes, I'm expected for Sunday dinner. But I've already missed it. You know that I'd rather be here with you?" Paul whispers into Jessica's ear, nibbling her soft lobe, offering a consolation now that she knows he is married. Paul knew he could not hide this fact forever.

He had seen these doe eyes before on women who had come to expect more from him in such a brief time. Jess is no different, and yet she is unique. Jessica wants Paul with a fierce immediacy, and she gives herself freely. *How glorious it feels to be desired!* Paul still has what it takes to please a woman. *What a high!* Paul soothes his guilty conscience: *Dinner is over anyway. He rarely misses this family ritual. Besides, Irini knows he has work commitments tearing at him these days.*

"Perhaps you can show me," Jessica is not letting Paul off so fast. She regards Paul's calm attitude and sense of throwing caution to the wind, and she likes it. She desires everything he represents: financial well-being and a family. Jessica wants the same loving couple relationship nurtured by her two doting parents. *Why is she settling for less with Paul? He has it all, and he is squandering his idyllic life. Or is it ideal? Why else is he here?* Jessica reassures herself that it *is* her; she attracts Paul like a bee to honey. *Maybe she can entice Paul away from his wife.*

Paul is lost in his reverie. *It feels strange. How can he want to be somewhere he has never been?* Jessica's apartment envelopes him in a private love nest: her carved queen-size four-poster bed contains plump linens, pillows, and throws. Abstract local art fills the walls. Candles and low lighting complement fresh flowers on a round wooden dining table; their fragrance permeates the whole place. Jessica's home is a tastefully curated country modern decor that reflects the complexity of contrasts like the woman inhabiting it. *Such a divergence from her stark office!*

"Your home is welcoming," Paul told Jessica.

"Thank you. It's my haven." Jessica responded, fluffing an artisanal woven pillow and tossing it at him.

Paul caught it as he scanned the living room with its plush loveseat and distressed wood coffee table, noticing the neat stack of *Cosmopolitan* magazines tucked into a bespoke shelf: "You read those?" He remembered when Irini bought one at the grocery check-out. She had scanned its articles about the ideal relationship and how to drive your man wild. *Was this Jessica's user manual? Because she has it in spades!*

"I leaf through them," Jessica was coy. "Come into the kitchen to choose your beverage." She changed Paul's focus.

Paul's ego is soaring. He knows he only needs to ask, and Jessica gives. Paul feels intense euphoria. This affair with Jessica contrasts Paul's mundane existence, and he muses: *Feeling wanted is heady stuff!* The struggle of working long hours and waking up to rinse and repeat each day feels mind-numbing.

Paul pulls Jessica onto the plush loveseat. She sinks

into the cushions, her hands resting on the bulge of his jeans. The fondling starts again.

"I'll be walking funny tomorrow," Jessica concedes as Paul lifts her skirt.

"Lie back," Paul commands. "You enjoy," he moves his lips over her femininity, kissing and nipping.

Jessica can do nothing but lie prone and relish the sensations of Paul's tongue flicking her clitoris while his fingers deftly probe her insides.

Paul feels like he is in heaven. He loves going down on a woman. Irini rarely lies still long enough for this pleasure. And it has been a while. He feasts until he grows stiff, and Jessica pulls him up to meet her need. They have sex for one last time today.

When Paul suddenly awakens from his post-coital snooze, he glances at his Cartier watch; it reads 9:25 p.m. He presumes his kids are in bed and Irini is writing. Paul tries to wrench himself away from the awkward sprawl of their twisted bodies on the sofa. Jessica is asleep. He picks her up and carries her to bed as she mumbles her request that he stay the night. Paul knows this cannot happen—not tonight. Jessica is snoring when Paul tiptoes from her room and lets himself out of her apartment, checking that the door has automatically locked. His legs feel like lead as he drives home. He is indeed satisfied.

◆ ◆ ◆

"I made a roast. Your plate is in the oven," Irini deadpans.

"I'm starving!" Paul's stomach reminds him that he spent so much energy making love with Jessica. He fears Irini is growing suspicious but calms his worries by digging into the delicious fare. "Mmm, you made it good!" he says between bites.

"You left your cell phone at the office. Apparently, I awoke a secretary when I called you," Irini states.

Paul panics and pats his pants pocket. His cell isn't there. *He'd left it on the nightstand at Jessica's, and Irini had awakened her, checking up on him!* "Yes, they were tired. We kept them late to work on the Ralston account. The new intern fell asleep on my office couch, and I didn't have the heart to wake her," Paul marvels at his quick thinking. It was fancy footwork even for Paul, who usually didn't go into the office on a Sunday.

"She won't have far to travel to work tomorrow," Irini scoffs. She recalls Paul telling her that the company pays the assistants well and would send them home in taxis when they worked late.

Irini is on her feet, clearing his empty plate and washing her hands. "I have a chapter to finish before coming to bed," She turns to leave the kitchen: "It's about my father's infidelity."

Ouch! "Thanks for keeping dinner," is all Paul can muster; his voice trails off as Irini leaves the room. He notices the rigid way Irini carries herself. Paul feels relieved that she's more eager to return to her writing than grill him about his activities.

Fourteen

Irini

Irini sits frozen, her pen poised above the fresh sheet of lined paper. She ruminates about Paul's lateness but knows she must delve back into her memoir. Irini scratches notes, reflecting on Katerina Kaminski's life as a mother:

Katerina peered into the face of the tiny pink bundle. It was all wrinkled and blotchy. She noticed a smear of yellow across the infant's forehead, the pasty residue of childbirth. *But how could that be? Look at this baby—she needs a bath!* Katerina had given birth enough to know that this child was not born in a hospital. *She was barely a day old!* Katerina's eyes narrowed as she probed Gino: "Where was she born?"

Gino shrugged. He could only remember his drinking buddy pulling him from his barstool, imploring him to follow; his favourite call girl was having a baby, and she claimed it was his. Too drunk to protest, Gino stumbled from the bar and up the stairs of the adjoining rooming house.

Gino had not even attended the birth of his children with Katerina; what could he do? When he got to Isabelle's cramped room—the one Gino had gone to countless times—a midwife was between the hooker's legs. All Gino could hear was cursing and panting, followed by guttural cries of his name.

"Gino, damn Gino! Where is he?!" Isabelle wailed.

"Shh. I'm here," Gino slurred the words that felt thick on his tongue after too many gins and tonics. He patted Isabelle's wet brow with his starched white handkerchief.

The girl baby's shrill wail echoed as the midwife caught her and swaddled her in a yellowed pillowcase. She handed the light bundle to Gino. He took the babe expertly as he had done with Irini and his children each time Katerina gave birth, and he was allowed to enter the room. Not knowing what else to do, Gino rocked Isabelle's newborn and cooed.

"Gin, she's yours!" Isabelle had told him. The room cleared of people, the walls closing in on him. *How did he never notice how tiny and dingy this room was?*

"How do you know?" Gino had asked her.

"Look at her, Gin! She has dark hair and eyes. I'm blonde. You were the only man I had sex with during those weeks. Remember? I was sick, and you told me you'd take care of me, that I shouldn't see other clients. You came every day for a month and nursed me back to health. I pleasured you. We made this baby, Gin. And I don't want her. She's yours. I don't have time for a child," Isabelle was on her feet now, pulling a ratty old bathrobe around her shrunken abdomen. She became faint, and Gino saw her wavering. He caught Isabelle as she was about to fall and laid her on the bed.

"Okay, I'll take her, Bel. I know a guy who can do the papers," were the last words Isabelle heard before she fell asleep, her robe tangled beneath her as she dozed atop the messy sheets.

The door to the cramped room opened, letting in a flood of light when the midwife returned with a bowl of warm water and a towel. She laid the infant on the wooden dresser and wiped her face amid new cries. She handed Gino a bottle of yellow milky liquid and told him to feed the squealing babe. Gino was good at that, so he complied. The smell of the suckling baby and the liquor on his breath created an odd pungent mixture.

Sobering up, Gino wanted to make things right. All he could think to do was bring the infant home to Katerina—she'd know how to handle a newborn. *Hadn't Katerina wanted more kids, anyway?*

◆ ◆ ◆

Gino was again between Isabelle's legs three weeks later, ready to penetrate her. He had a condom on; Gino would not make that mistake again, even if Bel were his favourite hooker.

"Go slow, Gino. It's my first time since having that kid. Is she okay, by the way?" Isabelle asked.

"Yes, she is safe with Katerina. Now shh...., Gino was eager for a release.

Katerina and Gino had named her Cassandra. They signed the legal paperwork the following week as Isabelle had promised. The two women never had to meet, which would have been humiliating for Katerina. Gino knew this: *There would be no forgiveness if Katerina found out the truth.*

Katerina had been confused, but she hadn't pressed for more details. Gino told her that the baby was his friend's love child and how she wanted a decent family for it. Katerina knew otherwise—she knew Gino was keeping the company of a whore. It gnawed at her, but Katerina felt powerless to change her circumstances with Gino. She convinced herself it was the juice— Gino would not be carousing if he weren't drinking. Katerina also reminded herself about the conditions under which Gino had married her: pregnant with a child she was raped into conceiving. Indeed, Katerina could forgive his transgression. Nurturing this child was her due; she would suck it up and repay Gino for taking in Irini.

Irini stands and stretches. All these memories are fusing, and she feels like she's spinning. She has an idea: she will create a memento box for Bella! Years from now, Bella will wonder about her roots and heritage. Irini can provide an essential start with photos and documented information.

She moves to the cupboard, retrieves family photos of Paul, the girls, Bella, and Cassandra, and sets them on her desk. Her hands make quick work of pulling and sorting images. Irini comes across a picture of a little boy in a sailor suit. He must be around three years old. *How cute!* She cannot stop staring at the image—there's a familiarity to it. *Who is this little boy that looks like Bella?*

Irini turns the photograph over and reads the faded blue ink: 'Paul Caldwell, age 3.'

"I'm tired. My eyes must be playing tricks on me," Irini mutters. She decides to continue this project later. She shuffles the photos into a pile and sweeps them aside. First, she must find a cookie tin for these keepsakes. She pads down to the kitchen, thoughts of the little sailor boy pushed to the back of her mind.

Fifteen

Irini and Cassandra

"Would you like herbal tea?" Irini pulls a pot from the high cupboard and searches through the boxed teas on the shelf below. She welcomes her sister's visit this quiet Sunday. Paul is working—unusual but more common these days—and the older girls are playing with their friends.

"Sure, peppermint if you have," Cassandra looks out the patio door window and settles her gaze on the dark curls bent over the shovel and bucket in her sandbox. Bella concentrates on her castle-making.

"Go on. When the tea is ready, I'll join you," Irini interrupts Cassandra's thoughts: "She'll be happy to see you."

Cassandra slides the heavy patio door open. Bella squeals with delight and barrels into her, sand flying from the shovel in her tiny pink fist as it clatters to the deck.

"Auntie Casssssssieeeeee!" the little girl pins Cassandra in a tight hug and plants wet kisses all over her face like a puppy.

Cassandra feels a warmth spread through her, unlike anything she experiences in her relationships with men.

"Come play with me," the child implores Cassandra.

"She's delighted you're here," Irini holds their cups and watches the scene with mixed emotion—pleasure and envy. She knows Bella's intense feelings for Cassandra come from a pure place.

"How about you show me what you're making, and I'll play in the sand with you next time? I'm not wearing my play clothes, Honey," Cassandra follows the little girl to the rectangular sandbox adjacent to the wooden deck.

Irini watches the mother and daughter interact. She observes their two dark heads of cascading curls, and the resemblance between Cassandra and Bella is like a magnet pulling together two positives. She notices how the child points with her shovel and shows her biological mother the different piles of sand in the various stages of construction. She hears Cassandra praise Bella's efforts while describing what she sees: "And you've made that one wide. I see a door and a tunnel." Bella beams, her smile as bright as the streaming sunlight.

"I'm going to sit with your Momma while you play, okay?" Cassandra returns to the shade of the deck and sits beside her tea: "She's so self-possessed, isn't she?"

"Oh, yes," Irini acknowledges. "Do you miss her, Cassandra?"

"Sometimes. But I know Bella belongs with you, Irini. I can't take care of her the way you and Paul do. Plus, she has your girls," her silky voice trails off.

"Bella is four now, and one day soon, she'll be old enough to know," Irini's face darkens as she recalls how their mother had told Cassandra the raw truth about her birth.

It had occurred during an argument when a local kid called Cassandra a bastard child, chanting it like a mantra. Everyone knew except Cassandra. She had come running into the house, crying over the taunts from her best friend's older sister, who was part of Lena's clique. The girl had pulled out the dictionary and read Cassandra the meaning of illegitimate child: "You were born to parents who are not married to each other," she'd pronounced with profound cruelty.

Cassandra understood that she was somehow different: "I'm one of those kids with no daddy, aren't I?" she had asked Irini, tears clouding her eyes.

Not wanting to make matters worse, Irini felt she had to correct Cassandra's perception based on what she thought she knew: "You have two parents who love you. The Mommy who had you could not take care of you, so our Daddy brought you here." Irini took the little girl into her arms: "You are like me, Cassandra. We are both special and loved," she explained, despite her own doubts.

Later that evening, Mama could not convince Cassandra that she was chosen like most adopted children are. Her reassurances were weak as she tried to mask her feelings: *I'm bloody cursed with not one but two daughters I did not choose!* As Cassandra grew older and asked more questions, Mama could not hide that she was the child her father had sired with a common whore.

"There won't be much to say, Irini." Cassandra went on: "Except that I made a mistake, and her real parents are you and Paul—that you *chose* her. She'll get over it the way I did."

"But did you get over it, Cassandra?" Irini asks.

"What are you implying, Irini?" Cassandra's face flushes, and her voice is sharp.

"Cassandra, the circumstances are similar," Irini says.

"They're not at all the same! You would never understand. Let's drop it, okay?" Cassandra rises from her deck chair.

Irini fears driving her younger sibling away with this talk, as she has done countless other times where Cassandra would go silent for weeks afterward. Irini feels insecure that Bella does not truly belong to her.

She yearns for it to be otherwise; Irini wants this little cherub to be hers with a fierceness that makes her womb ache—it feels like labour all over again. Irini wonders if there might be a similar pain in Cassandra's womb, one she may not know she feels. *Cassandra is soothing the ache with yet another relationship or conquest.*

"I want you to be part of Bella's life, but sometimes I fear you'll take her back someday. Is that bad?" Irini admits.

"Oh, Irini, I could never take Bella away from you! I know you love her like your own and want the best for her. If she comes to know me as anyone other than Auntie, you will always be her mom," And with that, Cassandra strides toward the patio door, empty teacup in hand. She is free to go, as she had come—Irini's constant bane as the surrogate mother to Cassandra's precious little Bella.

Cassandra kisses a busy Bella on the top of her sun-warmed head: "Bye, Precious."

"Bye, Auntie Cassie!" Isabella doesn't even look up from her castle-making.

Irini is on her feet: "Come by any time, okay? She misses you," Irini tries to ease her guilt as much as Cassandra's.

"No, she doesn't, Irini. I am merely the fun auntie who spoils her," she places a manicured hand on the patio door and pulls it open. Irini follows Cassandra, who lays her cup beside the sink and strides to the front door. "See you in two weeks, Rini!" She pecks her older sister on the cheek and rubs her arm. Irini must contend with the fall-out of her emotions as the front door closes. The revving of Cassandra's sports coupe matches her heart's palpitations.

Irini bursts into tears, thinking about the pain started by a broken, philandering father and ending in her own home. She cannot quite put her finger on the emptiness she feels inside. Still, huge sobs wrack her body, her chest heaving with a clenching in her heart that only a mother knows—crying for something she never knew she had lost.

A small voice jolts her: "Why are you crying, Mommy?" The innocent child in a sunhat, holding a shovel full of sand, asks Irini to explain emotions for which she has no words or honest answer. Irini scoops up the cherub-like girl and brings her back to the sandbox. She sits on the edge, tears drying, helping Bella construct a castle.

Sixteen

Jessica and Paul

Jessica and Paul lie prone in the grass, the fading mid-September sun warming their faces. They feel sated after a delicious picnic lunch she'd made for them. They watch huge puffy clouds float by, naming them and attributing their characteristics to physical objects. A decadent summer where Paul and Jessica had spent a month of long vacation days together, making love and taking day trips, is ending as they try to hold onto the holiday vibe of the season.

"Oh, look, Paul! That one resembles your profile," Jessica points to a cloud drifting overhead: "See the nose bridge and how the chin juts out like yours?"

Paul kisses Jessica. He has not had this much fun in a long time. Paul feels free on this gloriously sunny day, unconstrained, as though all his family responsibilities belong to someone else. Then he tickles her at the waist. Jessica squeals and begs him to stop.

"Make me," Paul commands.

Laughing and wriggling, Jessica says: "Stop, it's too much!"

"What's the magic word?" Paul continues.

"Please stop," Jessica pleads, serious now.

Amid her laughter, Paul continues his tickle attack: "You're sensitive today!" he notices.

Paul tickles harder, unrelenting. *He's in a devilish mood*, Jessica notes. He makes her beg: "What's the magic word now?"

Jessica begs and, between giggles, tells Paul she wishes he were ticklish, for she'd have no mercy. "Seriously, stop," Jessica is laughing deep from her belly.

"Nope. Paul corrects, "Wrong answer!" He continues his onslaught. Jessica feels the muscles in her abdomen aching and the pulling pressure in her pelvis.

"I'm pregnant!" she cries out.

Paul stops; his heart skips a beat. "You're pregnant?" He is incredulous.

"Well, you wouldn't stop. I needed to get your attention," Jessica's eyes twinkle merrily.

"You mean it's not true?" Paul's heart resumes its normal rhythm.

"Oh, it's true," Jessica confirms, still coming to terms with her excitement about the budding life inside her. She has contained the news, which astonished her because of what her gynecologist had pronounced about her fertility.

"When did you find out?" Paul sits up, growing solemn. His eyes narrow; he feels like he's learning a secret that everyone knows except him. It reminds Paul how, as children, his older cousins teased and taunted him about things only they were old enough to understand.

"I've suspected it for a while," Jessica looks smug.

Paul feels blindsided. "Jess, we've only known each other for three months!" he implores.

Paul does the math: Jessica had gotten pregnant the first weekend they met! *Gosh, they'd screwed like rabbits that Friday, then again Sunday.* And when he'd gone to retrieve his forgotten cell phone Monday evening, they had wild sex again. They'd practically clobbered one another, leaving a trail of clothes on the way to Jessica's bedroom. They'd done the deed twice that night and once more the following morning as he had relented and fallen asleep in her arms. They could not get enough of each other for the month after meeting. It was like a faucet had been turned on.

"So, when did you find out exactly?" Paul feels confused.

"Last week," Jessica says, the lie rolling off her tongue. She had suspected when she didn't get her period the month after they met, but she hadn't wanted Paul to know immediately.

"That makes you three months pregnant," Paul confirms.

"I'm due next April," Jessica informs, ahead of Paul, who is still processing the news.

"You don't take the pill?" Paul knows Irini takes her birth control pill like clockwork. She won't let him touch her if she has missed even one—not without a condom. He is kicking himself for being so irresponsible. Paul feels sure Jessica will not keep the baby as a single parent. *Besides, they barely know each other.*

Jessica is matter of fact: "My prescription had lapsed."

"Are you sure?" Paul feels like an adolescent boy who doesn't know any better.

"Sure of what, Paul?" Jessica sits up and looks him in the eyes: "That I'm pregnant or that it's yours?" Here was the calm, professional demeanour that had disarmed and attracted Paul, her boardroom persona presenting to all the pinched faces.

"Well, both obviously," Paul's tone is as dry as his mouth.

"I'm sure that I'm pregnant because I tested positive twice. And I'm sure this baby is yours because there have been no other men, Paul," Jessica furrows her brows and crosses her arms.

"We'll figure it out," Paul's voice cracks like a pre-pubescent boy, and here he is, almost fifty!

"There's nothing to figure out, Paul. I'm

having a baby next spring, and it happens to be yours," Jessica retorts.

The soft cooing Jessica now strikes Paul as a spider in whose web he feels inextricably trapped. *How could that be? Her prescription had lapsed. Did Jessica hijack him for his sperm? He had been willing.*

"You want to go through with the pregnancy, is what you're saying?" Paul double-checks, hoping he has heard wrong.

"It wasn't supposed to happen this way. I have a tilted uterus, and according to my gynecologist, I can't get pregnant easily," Jessica explains in answer to all the questions swirling around Paul's mind. "And yes, I want to have our baby," Jessica is firm.

Paul cringes at the thought of 'our.' *Can't get pregnant easily. What does that even mean? Has she been trying?* Paul recalls Jessica's evasiveness the first afternoon they'd met regarding her 'appointment.' He wonders if those flowers hadn't been a consolation. *He can't blame Jessica; she isn't a teenager. Indeed, her biological clock must be ticking. And he hadn't foreseen this outcome!*

Paul is so accustomed to Irini's careful planning that Jessica's spontaneity was refreshing. *How stupid of him!* Paul berates himself as Jessica cuts through his thoughts. She is lying on her back, caressing her still-flat belly.

"Oh, look, Paul! That one resembles a curled-up baby," Jessica points at a puffy cloud floating overhead.

Paul is no longer in the mood for this game. It has all gone horribly wrong from one cloud to the next. So wrong that when the sky darkens and the first spatters of rain send them rushing to gather up their blanket and picnic basket, Paul is relieved. He wants to go home and sort his thoughts.

The drive back to Jessica's apartment is quiet. She dozes while Paul listens to an Eagles CD on low volume. The summer sun fades into a purple-pink sky as Paul walks Jessica to her door. In a show of chivalry, Paul puts his copy of her key in the lock—the key she had readily offered after two weeks together.

Jessica had laughed when she said: "It's against sage advice to give my key to someone I don't share a lease with, but I've never followed impractical advice."

It was heady—Paul felt special! He had never held the key to another woman's place.

His cell phone rings; Paul plants a hurried kiss on Jessica's lips, surprised by the stirring in his loins. He manages to answer Irini's call on the third ring, stepping aside to let Jessica into her apartment. Paul turns to leave, and his chest heaves as if he had run a marathon. Paul recognizes his anxiety. He assures Irini that his meeting has ended as he sprints to his car.

"You sound out of breath," Irini observes.

"My phone was in another office," Paul lies. He's finding it easier to cover his tracks.

"And now it sounds like you're in a tunnel, Paul. There's an echo," Irini presses.

"Elevator's down; I'm taking the stairs." *God, why is she so perceptive? It must be the writer in her constantly trying to uncover pieces to puzzles,* Paul surmises. "I'm on my way, Irini. See you in twenty-five minutes."

"Supper's over," Irini is curt.

"Okay, well—" Paul isn't hungry anyway. The picnic lunch had filled him, and Jess' announcement had taken away any growing appetite—for food.

"I know the drill. Your dinner is warming in the oven. I'm going up to write. The girls will watch Bella until you arrive," Irini cuts Paul off, then she hangs up.

Paul hears Irini's icy tone. He senses she is running out of patience. He wishes Irini would not leave him Bella's evening routine. Not tonight. Paul wants to hide in his office. Everything is catching up to him, and Paul feels a great weight closing in. For a while, he will lay low. Jessica's pregnancy is new and isn't going anywhere. Paul hopes Jessica will miscarry. How often has that happened to women? Irini had miscarried a third and fourth pregnancy before they had agreed to stop trying to conceive a third child. Or it may be a colossal mistake—Jessica's period is merely late. That sometimes occurred with Irini. Paul's brain hurts trying to determine the myriad of variables beyond his control.

♦ ♦ ♦

"Daddeeeeeee!" Bella jumps on Paul as he enters the foyer of their sprawling two-story home half an hour later.

"Hey, Angel. Hi, Selena. Hi, Jenna." The girls look up from the television long enough to smile at Paul. They all have glistening wet hair from their evening baths.

"Girls, I'm beat. Would one of you read a bedtime story to Bella and tuck her in?" Paul begs.

Jenna, the nurturer like Irini, replies: "Sure, Dad." She pulls herself from the sofa, extending a hand to Bella.

"But I want Daddy!" Bella gripes and clings to Paul's leg.

"I'll come to kiss you later, Bella," Paul reassures his littlest one, who has a solid attachment to him.

Selena, the practical child, stands up and catches a squirming Bella: "I'll go with you, Jenn. Come on, tiny terror—bed. I'll race you!"

Paul feels grateful for his two older daughters. He enters the sanctuary of his office and closes the door. Paul sighs as he sags into his padded leather swivel chair and lays his forehead in his hand. A massive headache feels like a vice grip has him in a headlock.

Seventeen

Irini

Pen poised over paper, Irini sits in her attic sanctuary, spinning. Paul's continuing absences on Sundays tear at her. It has been months of late weeknights and weekends, missed dinners with leftovers warming in the oven, and Paul calling to say he's tied up in meetings. And no sex. Irini poses questions she had never entertained. *Was Paul indeed working? Or is there someone else?* She wonders, then chastises herself: *Paul works hard. How could she doubt that?* But it still nags at Irini as her thoughts return to the point in her memoir where she'd last visited: Katerina's suspicions about Gino's activities:

As if this baby Cassandra was not enough, Katerina found further evidence Gino was cheating on her. She sent Gianni to the bar one night to bring his father home. A drunken barfly pointed to the stairwell leading to a room above the bar. Gianni stopped short when he saw the tangled bodies of his father and another woman on the floor mattress. He ran straight home and, out of breath, told Katerina what he had seen: "Papa was lying naked with another lady."

Katerina had lashed out at Irini, "Your father is a lying, cheating bastard, just like you!" She sobbed into the sofa throw bunched around her: "What did I do to deserve this?"

Shocked to her core, Irini could not feel her own pain; instead, she ran to rest her head on her mother's heaving chest: "It's okay, Mama. You're going to be okay. We have each other," she soothed. Although she was only fifteen, Irini knew that Katerina was suffering. But Irini didn't realize that none of it was her fault. The stack of dominoes that fell into each other was because of events she could not control. Irini felt powerless to salve the depth of her parents' individual suffering.

Irini tells herself she is merely reacting to her mother's reality. *Or is she?* Irini contemplates the events; it dawns on her that family behaviours repeat themselves as though there is a template for others to follow. Irini is fascinated by how family legacies play out: *Unfinished business waits for closure, and the dysfunction stockpiles for the next generation to deal with.*

Irini turns it over in her mind; she's getting too close

to her characters. She settles on the reality of Katerina's life as a mother to her husband's child:

Katerina peered into the face of the innocent babe and reminded herself that this act of debauchery was not Cassandra's doing. "She will be a Caliani and grow up to be happy and productive," Katerina pronounced to Gino the next day when he was nursing a massive hangover.

"Sure," Gino was contrite. He knew he had dodged a bullet.

Katerina Kaminski was both smitten with and resentful of the exotic-looking child who was curious and friendly. Cassandra stole the hearts of most adults with the twinkle of her eye and tilt of her head. She'd sit in the guests' laps as they caressed her long silken hair. Friends would come for tea, and Katerina would find the little girl perched on them, telling fantastic stories.

On one occasion, Cassandra engaged a female visitor with a story about the fireflies she caught in a jar: "And I keep them in my bedroom; at night they dance in the dark like little fairies. My whole room lights up!" Cassandra broke into a song about magical fairies, her sweet melodic voice enchanting the woman so much that she cried and clapped her hands for a full minute. Mama had to take Cassandra to her room, for she was getting arrogant about her importance at this gathering, demanding even more admiration from the guests.

Cassandra basked in the attention from strangers,

something Katerina thought was odd. This child was fearlessly willing to trust people she didn't know. Katerina had tried to draw the line when Gino's friends came round, discovering how a growing Cassandra was particularly fond of doting men. Gino's friends would hold the beautiful little sprite in their laps for hours, knocking back shots and slurring lurid tales. Cassandra would listen with rapture and laugh, not knowing the meanings of their adult words and banter nor understanding the world from which they came.

Katerina cautioned the men as Gino guffawed at their tasteless jokes and colourful phrases: "You'll need to mind yourselves and your language around this young child!"

After the men left, unsteady on their feet, calling loud good-byes over their shoulders and cursing as they bumped into the garbage cans, Katerina would collect the empty liquor bottles. And she'd berate a drunken Gino for his lack of judgment: "Let Cassandra enjoy her childhood—she will soon belong to that world." The irony was twofold: Katerina's choice of words foreshadowed, and Gino didn't care because he was stuck raising a whore's child with whom he felt no bond.

Over time, at the start of these boisterous impromptu gatherings, Katerina would ask Irini to distract Cassandra. Irini would coax Cassandra into her room with the promise of a bedtime story. The curious child would interrupt the tale: "Tell me again about the lady who had a baby with no daddy. How come?" The precocious six-year-old Cassandra pressed for details about adult escapades.

"Sometimes it happens, Cassandra. But it's always better to have a daddy," Irini had explained as best she could. Irini felt the burden of describing the complexities of human relationships and romance to a child who had no clue she and Irini lived that same reality.

Cassandra was only fifteen the first time she became pregnant. It was 1975, and Irini was long gone from the Caliani family home. Irini recalls her shock when Cassandra told her: "I've missed two periods. I think I'm pregnant, Rini."

"Who is the father? Did you tell him?" Irini asked.

"I'm not sure," Cassandra shrugged.

"You mean you had sex with more than one person?" Irini could not believe what she was hearing.

"No," Cassandra lied.

"Cassandra, what is going on with you?" Irini pressed.

Cassandra was evasive. She would not say who had gotten her pregnant. And she did not want to discuss it. Irini felt anguish over abandoning Cassandra to fend for herself in the chaotic Caliani home.

Cassandra left school for a year to have her baby and arrange for adoption. By this time, twenty-eight-year-old Irini was married, thriving in her writing career and postponing having children until her thirties.

"You could come live with us and raise your child," Irini had offered Cassandra after talking with Paul. His career was taking off, so financially, they could help, and they had the space in their sprawling home. "It would let us see what it might be like having a baby around," Irini told him.

"It's not like sitting someone's dog for a weekend, Irini!" Paul had protested.

But he gave in when Irini reminded him that her sister needed a healthy, home environment during her pregnancy. Irini pointed out that taking Cassandra for six months would also help ease the burden in an utterly fragmented household. Lena had also gotten married, and Gianni was attending law school. Katerina and Gino could barely hold everything together by a thread, let alone nurture their teen daughter through her pregnancy.

"No," Cassandra was firm. "I'm giving the baby up for adoption," she asserted. "But I will stay with you until it's born."

When they learned Cassandra was pregnant, Katerina harped at Gino: "She's a little whore like her mother!"

Gino came to Cassandra's defense: "Accidents like this happen to teens, Katerina. And you would know, wouldn't you?"

"Irini was not an accident; she was a damnation!" Katerina cried.

He felt enraged: "Well, that damnation is taking Cassandra in because you refuse to mother your daughter!" Gino slammed the side door on his way out, leaving Katerina alone to fume.

"And neither of those girls are mine to mother!" Katerina spat into the echo chamber of the kitchen.

Irini had wondered if it had been heart-wrenching for Cassandra to give her baby to another family, like when the Calianis needed to rehome their pet kitten because of Gianni's worsening allergies. Irini had cried for weeks. Cassandra had cried, too. But Cassandra shed no tears when she left the Lakeshore General Hospital's birthing centre without her baby boy. Irini felt a loss, as though her sister's pregnancy was her own, and she experienced an emptiness: *I wanted something so badly for Cassandra that she did not want for herself.* Cassandra returned to live with Katerina and Gino and resumed high school, but not before Irini took the teen to her gynecologist and had him prescribe the birth control pill.

Irini considers the similar circumstances under which twenty-eight-year-old Cassandra brought Isabella to her and Paul. She had been evasive then, too. Irini knows that Bella will always connect to her roots because Cassandra is her birth mother; there is no information about Bella's father—Cassandra is unwilling to say. *Again!* Bella's mysterious conception weighs on Irini. Irini knows she'll have to field those queries one day, and she hopes Cassandra will have answers for the girl.

Meanwhile, Irini wonders if Cassandra sheds tears over the mother-daughter bond she will never allow herself to experience. Irini scribbles notes in the top corner of her page to revisit Cassandra's lack of maternal instinct and the eventual outcomes, to which she will have a front-row seat. Tears blur her vision, the words merging to look the same.

Irini rubs her eyes as a headache settles behind them. She is deep into the heads of her characters. Irini asks too many questions about her life, a life she's tried to do differently. This memoir remains her mother's story. Irini cannot afford to make the tale about her. *But isn't that what a memoir is?* She needs to get to bed to rise early for her reading tomorrow. Indeed, Irini's blind spot protects her; she has no clue how her life entwines with her mother's.

Irini pulls away from her desk and descends to her bedroom through the dark, quiet house. She knows Paul is still in his office, working. Irini feels she'd been too hard on him earlier. He worked today and still has loose ends to tie up at home. She is worrying about nothing. Still, something bugs Irini. And that nagging feeling persists through the night when she rolls over to the empty side of the mattress. Irini wonders why Paul has not yet come to bed, and she glances at the clock radio: 1:30 am. *Strange. He has an early day tomorrow, too.*

Irini rises to use the bathroom and hears Paul's muffled voice wafting from his study. He is talking on the phone. *Who could he be speaking with at this late hour?* Irini is tired but on alert. She knows Paul's work is consuming. *But still.*

Irini flushes the toilet to let Paul know she's awake. His voice stops. *Now maybe he'll come to bed.* Within minutes of tucking herself back under the sheets, the door creaks open, and Paul slips into the king-size bed.

"What's so pressing that you're on the phone at this hour?" Irini asks into the darkness.

"Oh, did I wake you?" Paul doesn't want to answer Irini after all he's been through these past twenty-four hours.

"No. I couldn't sleep—not very well," Irini says.

"Oh, one of the partners, Mike, works late. He told me I could call any time. We have an issue with the Ralston account," Paul's voice trails off.

He hates telling lies to cover up other lies. The truth is Paul had called Jessica to check on her and discuss how he reacted to the news of her pregnancy. He doesn't want her to feel abandoned, which she does; she spent their conversation crying. Paul called to ease his conscience, but Jessica kept him on the phone for over two hours!

He finally switched the subject to something enticing: "Join me when I go to the Bahamas next month for a conference," Paul offered.

"You're serious?" Jessica couldn't contain her surprise.

"Yes. Just you and me," Paul asked Jessica because Irini has a writing deadline and feels she cannot get away. Despite Paul's suggestion that her work is portable: "You could write in the mornings while I'm in meetings. We'd have the rest of the day together," he'd tried. "And we have our nanny, so the kids are covered."

"I'll pass this time, Paul," Irini said, "I'm deep into my creative routine. And there's too much going on with the girls. I need to be here for them."

He couldn't believe Irini was saying 'no' to a sunny vacation and the opportunity to reconnect!

"This will be good for you, Jess, and for us—time in the sun to relax and enjoy each other," Paul knew he was offering Jessica a second-place honour to buy himself time and gain credibility. He felt justified: *Irini had refused to join him.*

"That sounds decadent—yes, I'll come with you!" She didn't think twice.

Paul hung up after reassuring Jessica of his support and willingness to help with the baby. *Baby—he didn't know if he could do this all over again!*

"Paul?" Irini persists.

"Yes? I was falling asleep, Rini," Paul says. He tries to sound sleepy, like he'd dozed off rather than gone off in thought.

Irini softens. Paul hasn't used that endearing name

in a while. "Oh, well then, goodnight. Talk to you tomorrow," Irini kisses his shoulder. She hears Paul snoring as she rolls over to face the window. *He must be wiped.* She admonishes herself to be more compassionate and less mistrustful.

Irini cannot shake these tormenting feelings as sleep eludes her. An hour later, she dozes off, shady characters running around in her head. A nightmarish tale punctuates her fitful sleep: Paul is having an affair with Ms. Ralston. Cassandra caught them having sex in Irini's and Paul's garage. She tells Irini that it was all a mistake: Ms. Ralston was merely delivering files to Paul for a tight deadline.

Irini awakens alone in bed, sweating, her heart pounding. She feels groggy and disoriented. It takes time for her to land in her reality: the Ralston account is a dog food company owned by two gay men! Irini's subconscious is collecting puzzle pieces she has yet to assemble. Although tired, Irini prepares for her morning book reading at the local library. Sunlight fills the room with the promise of a bright day ahead. If ignorance is bliss, denial is blissful.

Eighteen

Bella and Irini

The butterflies are pretty in their frenetic movements, alternating flying and descending as the child follows them around the yard. *To be a butterfly!* she imagines, flinging herself across the grass, arms out, and propelling her body over the lawn, chanting, "I'm a butterfly! Look at me!"

It had been a year since Bella had gotten her new bicycle, and she was eager to ride it again this spring of 1993. "I'm almost five, Mom!" Isabella points out, trying to sell Irini on letting her ride alone.

"The rule is that you can only ride up and down the front walkway, Kiddo, while I'm doing yard work," Irini feels the compromise is reasonable. Bella agrees, grinning from ear to ear. "Please put your helmet on," she reminds Isabella.

Wiping her blonde hair off her sweaty brow with the back of her wrist, Irini stands to watch Isabella careen over the front lawn, alternating between riding her bike and running in the grass. *She cannot keep pace with the toddler's energy!* Irini looks up from her flower beds, her gardening gloves caked with thick black earth; she smiles and waves to Bella.

Irini surveys the tangle of vines through which budding white and yellow daffodils peek, heralding springtime and signalling renewal. She cleans the flower beds while the April sun warms the ground after the spring thaw. Irini bends to collect the gnarled weeds lying in the grass. She glances at the twisted debris, noting how the story in her memoir is also a jumble. "I'll pick those up later," she mutters and gazes at Bella, pedalling her little purple bicycle up and down the long walkway that divides their spacious front lawn. Her pink handle grip streamers fly in the wind, and Bella continues her 'butterfly' mantra in a sing-song voice.

The screeching sound of brakes mutes Bella's chanting. A silver sports car spins out of control as it takes the corner in a sharp turn and slams into the low rock garden wall bordering the Caldwell's walkway. A horrific crash shatters the sounds of childhood fantasy.

Bella's voice is a fever pitch scream as Irini tears toward her. Wedged between the front passenger tire of the car and the elevated flower bed is the twisted metal of the purple bicycle framing Bella's broken body. The pink bicycle helmet sits on the front steps. The driver slumps over the steering wheel, bloody and unconscious.

Distant ambulance sirens blare their impending arrival—confusion reigns. Irini is on autopilot; she kneels beside Bella: *If only I had been closer, watching her. And why is she not wearing her helmet?* "Hang on, Bella," she implores, "Please hang on," Irini mutters a prayer.

Perfunctory ambulance technicians extract Bella from the wreckage and load the little girl onto a backboard and into the vehicle. Irini robotically climbs into the ambulance. Through her dazed confusion, she hears a voice: "I'll wait for your girls to return from school. Your purse," the next-door neighbour drapes Irini's handbag over her arm as the doors clang shut. *This accident is surreal. One moment the child is carefree, pretending to be a butterfly; the next, she struggles to breathe in the cold technological interior of an ambulance.*

Irini braces herself for the heart-wrenching ride to the Montreal Children's Hospital Emergency Room, pleading for Isabella's life: "Please don't die, Bella. You're a butterfly, remember?" Irini sobs over an unconscious Isabella wearing an oxygen mask.

◆ ◆ ◆

Paul bursts into the room. Bella looks like a mummy; her bandaged body has tubes snaking into whirring monitors. A sombre Cassandra looks up from her hands, which she wrings in her lap. She sits on one side of the bed as Irini keeps vigil from the other side, stroking the little girl's bruised, bandaged forehead.

"He died. The driver died on impact," Paul announces. He had spoken with the police.

"Good, because I would kill him," Cassandra's deadpan voice cracks with a muffled sob.

"She's touch-and-go, Paul. They don't know yet," Irini mutters. She looks away from Paul's misting gaze as he approaches the little girl and touches her bandaged arm.

"She's asleep?" Paul asks.

"Unconscious—they told us the coma is a good thing because of the pain," Irini replies.

"How can there be any good in this? I never thought something could hurt this much," Cassandra shoots back." *Watching her flesh and blood suffer pains her more than anything she's ever experienced—more than giving birth to Bella.*

Paul is at a loss for words and feels he must say something to reassure Cassandra: "She's strong."

"I never thought I would feel this way," Cassandra shakes her head, a sob catching in her throat. "What if she doesn't make it?" she looks at Irini, black mascara smudging her eyes.

She's more fit a mother than I am! Irini wipes her raw cheeks, a wave of regret washing over her: *I could have done more to protect her. I was right there on the lawn when that driver plowed through.* Irini worries that Cassandra now wants to raise Bella herself.

As if reading her sister's mind: "It's not your fault, Rini." Cassandra shakes her head and sobs.

Paul nods to Irini, pulls Cassandra onto her feet, and leads her out of the room by her elbow.

"I'll sit by Bella in case she wakes," Irini is eager to be alone with Isabella and caress her forehead. Irini says a silent prayer: *Cassandra can have her back, but please let Bella live.*

Nineteen

Cassandra and Paul

"Yes, she's yours!" Cassandra hisses at Paul through her tears as they stand in the dingy visitor's lounge painted a pale, sick green, down the hall from Bella's room.

"I never asked, but I wondered," Paul admits.

"Well, so what? I would never tell Irini. I couldn't hurt her!" Cassandra spits, wiping fresh tears from her eyes.

Paul softens, "Seeing Bella with all those tubes must be hard for you."

"You have no idea, Paul. I carried her inside me for ten months," Cassandra cries. "Seeing Bella so injured is gut-wrenching! I don't know what will happen if—"

"—Shh," Paul hushes Cassandra, folding her into a warm embrace. He smells her hair, reminiscent of their fling five years earlier. Paul stops the memory in its tracks: *Now is not the time!* He rebukes his lack of restraint.

"I wish you hadn't told me that Bella is mine. Now I know, and that makes it more real," Paul sobers at the implications.

"It is real, Paul. You said so yourself that you always knew," Cassandra doesn't like Paul's selfish, self-protective attitude. She wants him to hurt the way she does. Paul can never know this kind of suffering because he's a man whose life is charmed. *How dare he complain about how real his dying daughter is!* Cassandra feels guilty about her selfish actions and resentful of Paul's bloated ego.

"This secret involves Irini," Paul worries about what this would do to her and them. "If she ever finds out—"

"Yeah, well, maybe it won't even matter!" Cassandra pulls away from Paul, goes to the window, and continues sobbing.

Paul offers a folded paper napkin from his pocket, the least he can do as he feels powerless, "Here."

Cassandra dabs her eyes, "You know this is why Gianni is holding off on the adoption."

"I had wondered about that, too," Paul says.

"How will you handle this with Irini?" Cassandra asks.

"I have no clue. Some things are better left alone, Cassandra," Paul is terse.

Cassandra's anger surges. She tastes bitter bile rising in her throat: *Fuck you, Paul!* Cassandra fights the urge to kick Paul in the balls. *That would clue him in about the pain she feels!* Instead, she decides to channel her anger into caring for Bella. Cassandra hastens out of the lounge.

"Besides, I love Irini," Paul mutters to himself. He feels guilt. Paul sinks onto the cracked fake leather couch in the dismal visitor's room to contemplate his fate. Although his undoing is imminent, Paul feels no remorse for his current recklessness, which is far from his thoughts. His life contains so many webs of untruth that entrap him.

Twenty

Jessica

A trickle of liquid gives way to a gush as Jessica grips the bathroom vanity for support. Searing pain rips through her pelvis. Her water is breaking. It is time to meet the little kickboxer inside who now wants out. *Oh, this freaking hurts!* Jessica wonders how she can go through with childbirth.

"Cassie, I'm in labour. Where are you?" Jessica implores into the phone, leaving a desperate voice message.

The plan was to induce Jessica tomorrow because she is one week overdue. But this morning, labour started; the baby is ready to enter the world on its own steam and terms. Jessica had given Cassie, her birth coach, the scheduled date five days earlier and watched as her friend circled it in her day planner. *How organized,* she had thought! Jessica felt relieved about

Cassie's support in keeping track. She had felt so alone throughout her pregnancy.

Paul was attentive; lately, they'd had lots of sex, which got the ball rolling. He could not get enough of Jessica during the last stage of her pregnancy. Before that, Paul was distant. He was non-committal regarding the birthing plan, let alone the life plan.

"Let's talk about when the baby is born," Jessica broached the subject one Saturday afternoon during her seventh month. They had enjoyed the wildest, most passionate sex, and Jessica was convinced Paul would move in and be a family with her and their baby.

"Jessica, let's just enjoy what we've got," Paul said.

"And what is that exactly?" she pressed. She was ready to know precisely where she stood with this man.

"We have fun together," Paul was being evasive. "And you know I care about you."

"You won't leave her then—your wife?" Jessica guessed.

"I didn't say that. But let's take it day-by-day. The baby is not even here yet. It's a little early to decide these things," Paul was backpedalling.

"I'm having your child in three months, and you find it too early to commit?!" Jessica was pacing her living room now.

"I am committed, Jess. I said I would help you with the baby's expenses," Paul defended himself: "I don't have to live here to do that."

"I'm not talking about here, Paul. We could get a house together," Jessica tried to reason.

"I already have a house. And I have a family," Paul reminded her—like she was a child who had forgotten a basic fact.

"And you'll have a family with me, Paul. What do you make of that?" Jessica knew she was playing the guilt card.

"We'll take it slowly, okay, Jess?" Paul wanted to end this conversation: *We're going in circles here. She wants a guarantee while I'm still figuring this out.*

Jessica accepted that Paul has a wife and children, but she doesn't like her role in the constellation of his double-life. Jessica worries about parenting alone. *But you knew that, Jess.* She chastises herself for harbouring hope.

Jessica takes no chances and calls for a taxi. The wrought iron bench beside the door holds her bags and nursing pillow prepared two weeks ago. She contemplates calling Paul, although it is a weekend—Sunday, no less. Jessica knows the drill. The man usually takes care of their youngest daughter while his wife sleeps late. *How can Paul dash out in the middle of this standing family obligation? But I'm having our baby!*

Paul had reassured Jessica that he would attend the birth: "You call me the minute you go into labour. No matter what I'm doing, I'll be there."

But that was when the baby was not imminent. The

kicking, discomfort, heartburn, constant peeing, and middle-of-the-night waking are coming to fruition. How could Jessica expect Paul to be anything more than a casual lover when he has a wife and children? She reminds herself of her earlier talk with Cassie, who suggested that Jessica have a baby on her own. She had protested, and now that reality is unfolding, Jessica feels like she's stranded on an island, unable to leave: *There's no turning back—I chose this route.*

Jessica had not wanted to tell her parents she was pregnant. When her pregnancy began to show, she stopped visiting. Jessica cited work commitments and how driving to Quebec City was too dangerous in the winter weather. Jessica worried her parents would judge her decision if they knew, and she wasn't ready to divulge her status.

As her belly grew under Uncle Francis's watchful gaze, Jessica lied to him: "My live-in boyfriend is shy and has not met my parents yet." She knows her father never speaks with his brother, Francis; their unique lifestyles are divergent.

"A woman needs her mother in times like these, Jessica. Rethink your plans," Uncle Francis had said, then he added: "I can't wait to meet this little slugger!" He was hoping Jessica would have a boy.

Jessica would sort things out once the baby was born. *Then her parents would embrace the child. They will be grandparents. What could be worse than that?*

Their unmarried daughter is bearing the child of a married man, that's what!

Another contraction rips through Jessica, reminding her to hurry if this baby is determined to be born sooner than her expected five-hour labour! She has forgotten to time her contractions, but they feel more urgent. Jessica calls Cassie again while waiting for the cab driver to ring her front walk-up apartment bell. She should have called an ambulance! The taxi company told her the cabbie would arrive in five minutes.

Oh, but where is Cassie? Cassie was supposed to meet Jessica at the apartment since they came from opposite ends of the city. Still no answer. She decides to leave a message: "Cassie, I'm on my way to the hospital—my water broke. Meet me in the maternity wing, please!" Jessica pleads.

Jessica consults her watch and glances at the bright baby corner with the bassinette and changing table she had set up in her bedroom—the bedroom where this bittersweet journey began last year with Paul. She had envisioned the homecoming: their new baby would sleep nearby for middle-of-the-night feedings while she and Paul slept in her queen-size bed. She imagined singing together as a family to Sharon, Lois, and Bram tunes like those on Paul's car CD player.

Contractions are ten minutes apart, and the taxi is still not here. Jessica regrets not telling her mother because she'd welcome her mom's support at this moment, assuring Jessica that everything will be all right. *What if she delivers now—right here?* Jessica panics: *Oh, hurry, please!*

The cab driver rings her doorbell, and Jessica locks her apartment and slowly descends the short flight of stairs. The cabbie glances from her rotund belly to the overstuffed weekend bag Jessica heaves, and he lurches forward to grab it.

Jessica shuffles behind, clutching her nursing pillow for comfort: "Don't worry; I won't give birth in your taxi!" she reassures the driver. But even she is uncertain.

Sighing relief, the taxicab driver throws the bag into the trunk and yanks open the back passenger door: "You lie down," he helps Jessica inside.

"I c-can sit!" Another contraction slams through Jessica as she slides into the warm interior of the running car and leans on her nursing pillow for support. The April weather is bitter cold. Jessica's coat falls open on her protruding belly. The designer label bouffant cut was a fantastic treasure from a local consignment shop. Jessica thought she might still find its styling suitable post-pregnancy if she is not sick of its ill-fit during these final weeks of looking like a hot-air balloon! Finding appropriate clothing to take Jessica through the various seasons of her pregnancy had been challenging because she hated the idea that there was no profit in this temporary investment. These maternity clothes were all going to the donation bin.

The taxicab wends its way through the quiet Montreal streets. There is no traffic this early Sunday morning when most people are home; Jessica knows it will be a tense drive to The Royal Victoria Hospital's Women's Pavilion. She feels every bump in the mottled city streets, aware that the passing winter has left giant potholes and gouges that any car ride would betray. The middle-aged ethnic driver looks with raised eyebrows in the rearview mirror: "Where's your husband, Ma'am?"

"Uh, he's not here right now!" Jessica doesn't want to explain herself to this driver whose religious beliefs may conflict with her reality—she had noticed the crucifix and rosary beads hanging from his rearview mirror.

"He gonna meet you there?" The cab driver asks.

"Yes, he's working. He'll come straight to the hospital," Jessica's voice catches as another contraction rumbles through her pelvis.

"Your husband works early on a Sunday. Is he a minister?" the cab driver persists.

Jessica wants to laugh at the irony, but she doesn't respond. She regains her composure and presses Paul's cell phone number on her mobile phone. The call goes to his voicemail: "Paul, I know it's Sunday morning. I can't reach my friend Cassie. My water broke, and I'm on my way to the hospital," Jessica closes her phone: *Well, at least he knows. I need him to know.*

The driver's furrowed gaze shifts to the rearview

mirror. Jessica closes her eyes and imagines a beach, its gentle waves lapping at the crystalline sand. The birthing instructor taught her how to use mental imagery during the throes of a jolting contraction and deep breathing, which Jessica must remind herself to do.

She recalls the first trimester of her pregnancy when Paul took her to a resort in the Bahamas for a conference he was attending in Nassau. The luxury hotel had little cabins on stilts at the water's edge. Jessica loved the gentle sea breeze, especially the romantic gauzy curtains that framed the ocean view. They'd made love every chance they could in their cozy tropical paradise, and Jessica did not want their travels to end.

"Come with me. It will be fun! You can enjoy the beach while I'm in meetings. They'll finish early, and we'll spend afternoons and evenings together," Paul's enthusiasm had sold Jessica on a decadent week alone as a couple.

How could she refuse? Besides, Jessica thought they might enjoy each other so much that Paul would move in with her right after the trip. Cassie's words about men never leaving their wives had nagged at Jessica; indeed, they had returned to their separate homes after a delightful week together. Still, Jessica was hopeful with each step they took. *Maybe when Paul meets their new baby, he'll move in.*

"We're here!" The cab driver cuts through Jessica's

meditation and reverie as another cramp sears through her.

The car stops, "The ride is free for you," the driver says.

Jessica thrusts two dollars tip into his hand and mutters, "Thank you" between clenched teeth as another contraction grips her. *Where is Cassie? Should she call Paul again?* Jessica feels abandoned!

An orderly removes Jessica from the taxi and seats her in a wheelchair, resting the maternity pillow in her lap and taking the weekend bag from the cab driver: "I wish you good luck and a healthy baby!" he gets back into his taxi.

A series of contractions rock Jessica's body as the aide rolls her down the long, winding corridor to the maternity wing. She closes her eyes to brace herself against the pain, murmuring curse words under her breath. She feels afraid of giving birth and scared of not giving birth!

The obstetrician-gynecologist hooks Jessica to a fetal monitor: "You decided to do this alone," the doctor states.

Jessica mutters, "No, *the baby* decided!" hit by a sudden, expected contraction.

"Breathe, Jessica," the doctor soothes. "Do you have a birth coach?" she asks.

"M-my best friend Cassie," Jessica says, "except I can't reach her. But I left a message," Jessica is hopeful.

She worries about her friend's silence: *It's not like Cassie to ignore her calls. Her cell phone is like a lifeline, especially for dates.*

The OB-GYN looks inside Jessica. "Our nurses will help you," she interjects. "You aren't alone, Jessica. Is there someone else we can call for you?" the doctor presses.

Jessica imagines how Paul would react if a medical staff person barged in on his Sunday morning: "Not for now. No." Despite her pain, Jessica protects the man responsible for her current state.

"Eight centimetres!" the doctor chirps.

"Wh-what does that mean?" Jessica panics.

"Get ready to push, Love," the nurse blots Jessica's sweaty brow with a cool cloth. "At ten centimetres, the magic number."

"But it hurts so bad!" Jessica wails.

"I'm stepping out for a minute, and when I return, we'll go for it, Jessica!" the doctor snaps her gloves off, discards them in the trash can by the door, and leaves the room.

Jessica feels new panic grip her. A cold sweat breaks out as another, more persistent contraction rocks her pelvis, willing Jessica to push. She begins panting and pushing.

"Wait!" The nurse admonishes, "The doctor is coming to deliver your baby."

"Hold off? What the fuck?!" Jessica mutters, "I

c-cant!" and pushes again as the OB-GYN hurries into the room.

"I'm back. I'm back! Okay, Jessica, push!" the doctor coaches Jessica. And with that, light hair crowns between Jessica's pale thighs, followed by a pair of shoulders, then the rest of the baby. The OB-GYN expertly catches the slippery infant.

"You have a little girl, Jessica!" The doctor cheers. She clears the baby's mouth and ensures normal breathing. She holds the newborn up for Jessica to see. The infant wails, and Jessica feels relieved. The doctor cuts the cord and seals it into a pre-labelled plastic bag per Jessica's and Paul's signed agreement to preserve the cord and its precious stem cells and blood in case of a future need. A nurse rushes it out of the room while Jessica's baby undergoes measuring and Apgar testing to evaluate her health. Jessica slumps back into the pillows and closes her eyes.

Cassie runs into the room: "Oh, Jess, I missed the birth, didn't I?" She is out of breath.

"She's beautiful, Cass," Jessica is exhausted but blissful. "I had her moments ago."

"I am so sorry," Cassie hangs her head.

"I couldn't reach you for the past few days. And labour started this morning." Jessica notices how dishevelled Cassie looks, not the Cassie who appears made-up and wearing heels and trendy clothes. Her friend looks unkempt in sweatpants and a tee-shirt, hair in a messy bun, and bloodshot eyes rimmed with dark circles.

"There is so much going on right now," Cassie considers explaining. *No, not when Jessica is experiencing maternal joy.*

"It's alright—oh, here she is!" Jessica's arms reach for the swaddled bundle.

The nurse is perky when she announces the infant's perfect Apgar score: "Your little girl is eighteen inches long and weighs seven-and-a-half pounds."

Jessica is relieved once more.

Cassie looks at her friend in awe; a glimmer of understanding dawns on her: "She's fair like you!" Cassie exclaims.

"Her dad is blond, too!" Jessica beams.

Paul bursts into the room carrying a bouquet of daffodils: "Jessica—" he stops short when he sees Cassie cooing at his daughter.

"Paul! Come meet your little girl!" Jessica beckons Paul over to her bedside: "And this is my best friend, Cassie!" She looks from Paul to Cassie, instantly realizing they know each other.

"We've met," Cassie's tone is icy.

"What do you mean?" Jessica's face contorts with confusion.

"So, you're the Baby Daddy?" Cassie spits at Paul.

Paul stammers, "And you're Cassie, Cassandra?" He feels exposed and anxious.

"Cassandra??" Jessica looks from Paul to Cassie. She's only ever known Cassie as Cassie: "I-I don't understand. How do you two know each other? Paul?" Jessica presses.

The infant starts wailing, and the nurse rushes in: "You need to leave for a wee bit. We must get this angel feeding." She is matter of fact, pulling the curtains around the bed and closing Cassie and Paul outside. Paul slips the bouquet onto the bedside table through a slit in the drapes and ducks out, grabbing Cassandra's arm.

They find themselves again in a hospital visitor's lounge down the hall, its bright walls sporting pictures of nursing infants, in stark contrast to the one on Bella's ward and the moment's mood.

Cassandra hisses: "You get around, don't you? My best friend, and you're the father?! I can't believe it, Paul! You amaze me!" she spits.

"Cassandra, wait! I fell in love with Jessica!" Paul explains.

Cassandra is roiling now: "*Love*, Paul? During her pregnancy, all I heard was how you were a married family man, and Jessica must guard that, or she might not have you in her baby's life! And my sister, Irini, is innocent in all this. Does *she* know, Paul?"

"I don't think so," Paul musters. "I've been discreet."

Cassandra scoffs: "And careful, I can see! Have you ever heard of using a condom?"

"Like when you jumped me five years ago?" Paul shoots back. He wants to hold Cassandra accountable.

She is livid: "You never stopped me! And now Irini is fighting for the child resulting from that sexcapade!"

"Anyway, let's focus on what's important here. Bella needs her mother right now," Paul states.

"What Bella needs is a lifeline, Paul! She's suffering life-threatening complications. Our baby is dying, Paul!"

"I wish I could do more," Paul feels helpless.

"And here you are, a humping sperm donor! My best friend, Paul—Jess is my best friend! How come I had no clue it was you? Jess never mentioned your name during those ten months. She was protecting you, Paul! The same way I did when I gave birth to Bella!" Cassandra paces the room, frustrated at witnessing her best friend going through what she had experienced years earlier. Cassandra knew otherwise, but she had let Jessica entertain her fantasy, especially since Paul could have been anybody—certainly not the Paul to whom she is related! The only difference is that her friend still harbours hope of winning Paul and creating a happy little family.

"They never leave their wives! I told Jess that all the time! Are you planning to leave Irini, Paul?" Cassandra is indignant, jabbing her fading manicured finger into his chest.

"No, I love her!" Paul bows his head.

"And showing it by making babies with not one but two women! Are there any others, Paul?" Cassandra probed.

"No," he winces, realizing his near misses with casual sex partners. They would come to him concerned about missing pills and having late periods. One woman had taken the morning-after pill. Paul had arranged for another lover to have an abortion; he stayed to ensure she was okay but never saw her again. It had scared Paul enough to make him take a hiatus from his philandering. But then, three months later, Jessica happened. And he had grown to love her. "No others," he assures Cassandra, his furrowed expression belying his distress.

"What do I tell Jess when I go back there, Paul? That we both have babies by you?" Cassandra implores.

"Let her enjoy her newborn. We'll sort this out when things settle down," Paul regrets the path of lies and betrayal he is on.

"But she'll want to know. And on top of that, I missed the birth! I was supposed to be Jessica's birth coach, but I kept vigil by Bella's bed! Do you have any idea how that feels? My baby is dying while my best friend delivered a healthy little girl. What do I tell her, Paul?" Cassandra demands, knowing that Paul has no more answers than she.

"Just tell Jessica that we are related. Does she know about Bella?" Paul asks.

"No. But I wanted to tell her! Because through all this, Paul, I have realized that I ache for that little girl in a way that I never thought possible! What do I do with that, Paul? I cannot even share it with Irini! Not now. Not ever!" Cassandra cries.

"We can go in together and tell Jessica the minimum. After that, what you do is up to you," Paul offers, hoping Cassandra agrees and will continue to protect him.

"Alright, but I can't stay long. I want to go back to my daughter," Cassandra wipes the tears from her eyes and pulls out a compact to check her face.

They walk back to Jessica's room like two strangers, on opposite sides of the hospital corridor. Jessica sits up in bed; the swaddled baby is suckling. The new mother beams. "I'll call her Eva for 'life,'" Jessica announces, forgetting the strangeness that had transpired earlier.

"That's a lovely name! She's beautiful," Cassandra starts gently: "Jess, Paul is my brother-in-law."

"I'm shocked," Jessica's voice trails off. She doesn't press for more details. Tears well in her eyes.

"I had no clue, Jess. You talked about Cassie, but I never made the connection," Paul interjects. He hands Jessica a tissue, something he often does with women these days.

Jessica wipes her wet cheeks and brushes the air like she's casting the reality away. She turns her attention to her infant: "Isn't our daughter gorgeous, Paul? Look—she has your blue eyes."

Paul's stomach flip-flops as he bends to kiss Eva, savouring the bittersweet moment while feeling a guilty lump in his throat. He pledges to right all his wrongs. *But how?*

"Jess, I'll let you get some rest. I must go now," Cassie says.

"But you just arrived!" Jessica protests. She feels shortchanged because Cassie was supposed to be with her throughout the delivery.

"I have a family matter, Jess, and I need time. It was unexpected. I'll tell you more about it soon," Cassie plants a kiss on the now-sleeping Eva's forehead, squeezes Jessica's shoulder, and leaves.

Jessica cannot help but wonder if her friend is lying and has a hot date. Then a wave of guilt washes over her for suspecting Cassie would rather be with a man. Cassie does appear distracted and is not her usual glamorous self. It makes Jessica wonder anew. Jessica couldn't imagine Cassie running to a date looking unpolished. "Okay, see you soon," Jessica calls as Cassie sprints from the room.

"She seems rushed," Jessica turns to Paul, "How are you two related again?" She has a clue, but Jessica wants to hear him say it. She caresses the soft downy hair on her daughter's head.

"Cassandra is my sister-in-law," Paul sighs.

"So, that makes it by marriage. Cassie isn't married, though. Is she your wife's sister?" Jessica confronts Paul.

"Yes, her youngest sister," Paul admits.

"Ah, that's awkward. Will Cassie tell your wife?" Jessica hopes their secret will blow wide open and pave the way for Paul to become a family with her and Eva.

"No. We talked about it. Our relationship is complicated. And now, with Eva…." Paul cannot say 'our daughter' because he does not want to give Jessica any illusion that they are a family. *However, their relationship is a forever one!* Paul feels cornered.

"Paul, you said you'd take care of us—Eva and me," Jessica panics and reminds Paul of his earlier promise.

"I know, Jess, and I will. The timing is bad," Paul's brow furrows, a hint of fatigue in his usual relaxed tone.

He looks frazzled and messy like Cassie—or Cassandra. Strange. Jessica cannot put her finger on it.

"Yes, the timing is unfortunate for our baby, who you knew was coming this week," she snipes. Then Jessica softens: "Paul, is everything alright?" She wonders if the family issue Cassie mentioned is also affecting Paul. That would make sense. What doesn't make sense is Jessica's burst bubble about baby making three. And she's still trying to accept that Cassie is related to Paul—his wife's sister, no less!

"I wish I could say 'yes,' but you just gave birth. You must rest. Look, I'll come by later. You get some sleep." Awash with guilt, Paul kisses Jessica's forehead and runs a fingertip down the bridge of Eva's nose—*another girl!* "Good night, ladies!" and he is gone.

It feels as if Paul had never come. Jessica glances at the white daffodils on the bedstand and feels hopeful for a fresh start. She rings to ask the nurse for a container.

Jessica peers at her daughter: *she never wants to let this little cherub go.* Eva's shrill cries pierce the stillness, and Jessica knows the infant is hungry again. She prepares to breastfeed her baby for the second time since birth. *Is she already bonding?*

Twenty-one

Two Mothers and Paul

"Are you Isabella Caliani's mother?" The young woman in a white coat with coloured buttons and ribbon lapel appliqués asks.

Both women look up simultaneously from either side of the bed. They recognize her as the doctor assigned to Bella. It's been two days of tests, and now they may finally get answers.

Irini and Cassandra exchange glances, and Irini says: "We both are."

"I'm her biological mother," Cassandra corrects, "and Irini has custody of her."

"I'm Dr. Sauvé, the pediatric emergency physician for Isabella. Your little one's suffered a trauma. She looks from one woman to the other as Paul hurries into Bella's room right after meeting newborn Eva. Dr. Sauvé turns to him: "And you are…?"

"Bella's father," Paul sighs. The truth of this statement has never been more accurate.

"Okay, good, then we'll have to assess each of you," Dr. Sauvé announces.

"For what?" Paul goes white.

"Your little girl has a blood disorder. We've determined that Isabella needs a donor treatment—bone marrow," Dr. Sauvé explains.

Irini asks: "Are you telling us that you need bone marrow from a parent?" She looks from the doctor to Cassandra with a hopeful expression.

"Yes, or from a sibling. Unless, of course, you saved the cord blood as some parents do nowadays. We have better chances with stem cells, even from a sibling," the doctor focuses on the three pairs of eyes staring at her.

"Cord blood," Paul mutters. He recalls how Jessica wanted to bank the baby's cord blood and tissue. Paul had prepaid the hefty sum for an eighteen-year storage plan and co-signed the papers months ago.

Both mothers exchange looks. The walls close in on Paul; the doctor's voice is a distant drone in his ears.

"Cassandra?" Irini touches her sister's arm, "Did you by any chance?"

"No, but I can still be tested as a donor, right, Doctor?" Cassandra's eyes are more sunken than Irini had ever seen them. She understands the weight on her sister's shoulders.

"Yes, we'll do a requisition right away. Time is critical," Dr. Sauvé's eyes soften as she smiles. "And her father?" she persists, looking at Paul.

"I'm not sure I know his whereabouts," Cassandra's face reddens as she protects Paul again. *Or is she protecting herself? No, right now, she's protecting Irini.* She could not bear to cause any more pain to the woman tearing herself up with guilt about the accident that left little Bella lying shattered in the hospital bed.

"If you could track him down—we want to expand our chances of a perfect match." Dr. Sauvé perseveres: "And does Bella have any siblings?"

Irini looks up as a veiled glance passes between her husband and her younger sister. They all shake their heads in unison, and Irini says, "No."

"We must move quickly, then. I'll prepare the requisitions. Do you have any questions?" Dr. Sauvé smiles.

"None for now," Cassandra chokes back a sob as Irini moves to console her sister.

The doctor prepares to leave the room, and Paul rises after her.

"Paul?" Irini looks up from Cassandra's shoulder.

"I'll be right back," he says. Irini hears Paul call out to Dr. Sauvé in the hallway, wondering what question he might have.

Twenty-two

Paul

Paul catches up with Bella's pediatrician: "Uhm, Dr. Sauvé, can I meet with you privately?" Paul notices dark lashes framing pitch-black eyes under a tumble of long, wisped bangs of the same exotic colouring. *Now is not the time for come-ons,"* he reminds himself.

"Yes, Mister….?" Dr. Sauvé wonders about this man with a distinguished demeanour despite his unkempt look.

"Caldwell. I am Isabella's father. You can call me Paul," he stammers.

The doctor raises her eyebrows.

"Yes, her real father," Paul elaborates.

"Okay, step inside my office," Dr. Sauvé waves him toward a door down the hall. Her tone is professional.

Paul wonders how Doctor Sauvé would look naked. He envisions her white coat and stethoscope lying on her office floor, playing doctor with the Doctor in a strange twist of events.

Paul sits opposite Dr. Sauvé as she retrieves a manilla folder marked 'Isabella Caliani.' He pictures Dr. Sauvé nude and willing atop her mahogany desk.

"So, tell me about the family tree, Mister Caldwell. I'm confused," Dr. Sauvé flashes Paul an ironic smile that plays across pink-glossed lips, revealing straight, gleaming teeth. Paul imagines tasting a mouthful of those plump lips, biting and kissing them.

"Mr. Caldwell?" The doctor pierces his fantasy.

"Yes," Paul jolts back to reality.

"The family connection?" Dr. Sauvé probes.

"Right. Can you assure me of client confidentiality?" he asks, his brow furrowing. Paul fears he's gotten himself in way too deep.

"To a point," the doctor's voice is professional now, its iciness slicing through any warm thoughts Paul was entertaining. "Why don't you lay it on the table, Mr. Caldwell?" *How fitting!* Paul muses about his earlier fantasy.

"As Cassandra is Bella's birth mother, I am Bella's biological father. Cassandra and I are not married. You understand? My wife has no clue," Paul's admission sounds shameful to his ears. But he has no time for self-recrimination.

"I see," The doctor says. "Look, I'm not here to judge you, but we have a deathly ill child, and if you're a match, Isabella's chances are better."

"And if neither of us is a match?" Paul assumes the worst. He has always been a realist; it makes him a keen negotiator.

"Well, then we cast our net further." Dr. Sauvé presses, "Do you have other children, Mr. Caldwell?"

"Yes," Paul hesitates. He considers his two oldest daughters, then Eva.

"But they're with your current wife, who has no clue. I see how this is problematic. Consent, you know," The doctor's voice softens. And Paul becomes hard again at the thought that there is one hot woman under this cold professional veneer. He mentally chastises himself for entertaining the idea.

"Exactly," Paul feels defeated; he worries that he won't be a match. And selfishly protecting his double-life, he has decided against suggesting to Irini that one of their daughters might be a donor match. Paul calms himself: *One step at a time.*

"Well, Mr. Caldwell, you could do what makes you happy, or you could do the right thing. I'll leave that with you. In the meantime, we'll be able to assess you confidentially. And the birth mother, of course," Dr. Sauvé turns to her paperwork: "If you'll excuse me, I must write up the forms."

Dr. Sauvé tells Paul which room to report to the

following day for his test, indicating the bold writing on the form ensuring his confidentiality. He leaves the doctor's office, heaving a sigh of relief. Paul has been granted a reprieve. He doesn't expect any second chances; his mind tries to navigate the uncertainty.

As he steps out of the doctor's office, Paul sees the elevators, and on impulse, he presses the button for the main floor. He will take a taxi to the Royal Victoria Hospital, about two kilometres away. Paul has not gone to see Jessica since she gave birth yesterday. He feels awash with guilt, combined with the emotional heaviness of all the responsibilities he is currently juggling: a new life on the one hand and a life in the balance on the other. This unfair irony does not escape Paul.

During the cab ride through the thick downtown traffic, Paul prays that Bella is not the sacrificial lamb for the sin he committed by conceiving Eva. *How ludicrous!* he concludes. *Jessica had decided to keep this baby.* Paul only promised his financial support. But Paul hadn't counted on all this baggage as part of the deal.

And why did Cassandra have to tell him Bella is indeed his? It was easier not knowing, even if he had suspected. What had he done to push Cassandra into telling him? Surely, now she'd want to have her child back. Hell, he'd have to support her, too! He'd have to take care of three families—whether Irini discovered the truth or if he told her. The doctor's words play heavily on his mind: What is right in this mess he's created?

Paul enters the lobby of the Royal Victoria Hospital and squeezes his way through the crowd of people in the elevator. Distracted by his thoughts, he ends up in the basement. "Damn!" Paul mutters and re-enters the elevator. He exits on the main floor, thinking it is his stop. Suddenly, Paul is standing amongst the pinched-faced partners of his firm. They hold an assortment of fragrant flowers, pink balloons, and stuffed animals.

"Uh, Gentlemen," Paul stammers; he feels confused. He only told the office he needed time to deal with a family emergency. Indeed, this is a strange mistake. Had Irini spoken with them about Bella during a call when she'd dashed home to shower and change clothes? Paul has his hospitals mixed up. *No, this is the Royal Victoria Hospital,* he reminds himself.

"Paul, fancy meeting you here!" the most senior member booms, slapping Paul on the back.

"Likewise! Is that for—?" Paul stops short.

"—Yes, yes, for our favourite PR person, Jessica. She had a baby. And we want to give her our congratulations, of course! Why don't you join us? Is that why you're here, too?" The oldest pinched-face claps Paul on the back again, like he is burping a baby.

"I'll go another time," Paul hesitates. "I have personal business to deal with." He wonders to himself: *Do they know?*

"Are you well, Paul? They told us you have a family emergency. Is Irini all right?" The oldest one queries.

"Yes, she's fine. Our youngest daughter had a little accident," Paul makes it sound banal not to arouse their interest. His brain can't deal with their reactions.

"We hope she'll be fine," the pinched-face soothes.

"We do too. I must run. See you soon!" Paul is eager to leave the group of older men looking at him with penetrating eyes: *Like they know something.*

"Give Irini our best. And good luck with your little girl. Kids often get into the darndest situations," he says.

Paul wonders if the old pinched-face is going senile.

"We'll give Jessica our best on your behalf. Mike signed your name on the card," he informs Paul.

"Thanks!" Paul cannot leave fast enough. When the doors open to whisk the men away, he ducks into the corridor facing the elevators and sees the arrow sign marked *Cafeteria.* Paul could use a cold drink.

Paul decides to visit Jessica this evening when Irini falls asleep by Bella's bedside. *They have so much to discuss regarding how Eva can help Bella.* Meanwhile, it will look odd to Jessica that Paul had 'signed' the company's congratulations card. Paul hopes she doesn't notice.

Twenty-three

Three Sisters and a Brother

Irini looks up from where she keeps vigil by Bella's bed. The child is asleep, resting well after her life-saving procedure, and her colour has returned. Cassandra dozes in a chair on the other side of the bed.

Suddenly, Lena and Gianni burst into the small room, carrying gifts.

"We heard! Oh, Irini, how is she?" Lena rushes to the bedside as Cassandra awakens, sitting upright from her slumped posture in the cramped chair.

"I told Lena when Cassandra called me. We wanted to be here for you," Gianni explains their visit. He places the gift bags on the wide window ledge for Bella to open when she awakens.

"We think she has a good chance. They gave her donor stem cells," Cassandra says groggily.

It had been a harrowing week, and they were still snatching sleep whenever they could. Irini had insisted they take turns going home, but Cassandra wanted to stay by Bella's bedside. When she wasn't keeping watch herself, Irini did her best to bring food and changes of clothing to her younger sister.

"One of our parishioners whose daughter recovered from leukemia had this treatment, and it worked," Lena shares. "Medical technology is wonderful! But God is merciful and works miracles."

"It's a new procedure, so we must wait and see, but it looks promising," Irini is hopeful.

"She looks so peaceful and beautiful," Lena touches Bella's forehead: "Hey Girl, it's Auntie Lena. You have cousins to meet, so please get well soon!"

"It will take several months, but Dr. Sauvé expects Bella to recover fully because she is young and strong," Cassandra explains.

Gianni interrupts: "This may not be the right time, but do you still want to go through with the adoption?" Gianni looks from Cassandra to Irini and back to Cassandra.

Lena glances at Gianni, her eyes darkening: *How insensitive of him to mention this now! What is he thinking?!*

Irini turns to Cassandra. They had not revisited Irini and Paul's adoption of Bella for several years, and now, Irini's worst fears are coming to the fore. With the accident, the decisive moment is upon them.

Cassandra smiles reassuringly. She remembers her conversation in Gianni's office three years ago when Irini reminded her about their agreement to finalize Isabella's adoption:

"Do you know who the father is? Because I must do a paternity check before we draw up the adoption papers. The father must sign off," Gianni informed Cassandra.

"What if I tell you to forget about the father?" Cassandra asked.

"Well, do you know who he is?" Gianni pressed.

"And what if I do?" Cassandra hedged.

"He needs to sign. Does the father agree to this adoption?" Gianni tried again.

"It's complicated. Can we put me down as the mother and leave it at that?" Cassandra asked.

"Cassandra, what are you not telling me? Look, I'm a lawyer—Client-Attorney privilege. I can assure you total confidentiality," Gianni's tone was conciliatory.

"No matter what?" Cassandra asked.

"No matter what," Gianni affirmed. "I'm not interested in conception politics."

Cassandra decided to tell him the raw truth: "Gianni, Isabella's father is Paul."

"Paul who…?" It dawns on him: "Oh, that Paul!" Double-checking what he'd heard: "Irini's Paul? Look, no judgment, but does she know?" he asked.

"No, and I want to keep it that way," Cassandra warned.

"Paul cannot adopt a baby that is already legally his. Irini would need to adopt her, though. Does Paul even know?" Gianni asked.

"I've never told him, but he has an idea. Paul and Bella share a close bond. She even looks like him," Cassandra winced. "So, can we just forget it? Please. Let's leave well enough alone."

"Do you think Irini suspects it?" Gianni is concerned about what this knowledge would do to his older sister, especially given their history.

"I don't think so. Irini is busy writing," Cassandra worried that Irini wondered—how could she not—but was in denial. *That would be more likely.*

Gianni didn't believe this triangle he was witnessing: "You and Paul…are you a thing?"

"No. Paul and I had a fling—it happened once," Cassandra clarified.

Gianni sucked in his breath, making a whistling sound, and shook his head: "Up to you, Sis, but it can get messy with time. What happens if rumours fly when Bella is old enough? Like they did with you."

"It's not going to happen," Cassandra was hopeful, although she remembered the cruel taunts.

"Cassandra, these things have a way of bubbling to the surface. Are you sure that you know what you're doing?" Gianni pressed her.

"It's already done, and I can't take it back. Try to put Irini off when she calls you about the adoption. We'll revisit it when we need to," Cassandra stood firm.

◆ ◆ ◆

"Can I see you outside for a moment, Gian?" Cassandra rises and beckons her big brother to follow her into the corridor. Irini exchanges a worried glance with him and nods: *Is Cassandra ready to finalize the adoption?*

They leave the room, move away from the entrance and speak in hushed tones.

"Gianni, Bella is my daughter. Her accident has shaken me to my core! I'm not ready to ignore that fact," Cassandra's eyes mist.

"You mean you want to take back custody?" Gianni asks, "Anyway, Bella is legally yours."

"It's all new to me. I'm adjusting to what maternal love means," Cassandra shares. She's not ready to be a full-time mother, but Bella is her flesh and blood, and now she feels it.

"So, you've told Paul Bella is his?" Gianni guesses. Cassandra nods.

"Well, give it time, Cass. Bella is still recovering. See how you feel when she returns home," Gianni is optimistic that Cassandra and Irini will work things out for Isabella's best interests. He's seen custody suits before but never an adoption retraction, notably since the arrangement was not legalized. *And this is family. Blood can undergo severe tests regarding complex matters of the heart.*

Gianni and Cassandra re-enter Isabella's room. Irini and Lena are deep in conversation as if they had never been apart. They are catching up, comparing mothering stories, and making plans to reunite the cousins this summer.

"There's so much to be grateful for!" Irini beams. Bella has survived, and Irini feels she has come full circle with her estranged sister.

Epilogue

"Would you please sign mine?" the sweet voice asks.

Irini is wrapping up a book signing at her local independent bookshop for the spring 1994 launch of her newly released memoir, *Legacy of Lies*. The stream of family, friends, and fans has tapered off. Irini is about to pack up and call it a successful event. Instead, she retrieves the engraved Montblanc Paul had gifted her when she published her first novel.

Pen poised, Irini asks: "And what shall I write to whom?"

"Jessica," says the young woman with a strawberry blonde ponytail, stray wisps of hair framing her beautiful features. She jostles on her hip an adorable baby with piercing blue eyes.

That cherub face reminds Irini of Isabella—beautiful Bella, six years old and thriving since her horrible brush with death. Irini could swear she was looking at a younger, fair-haired version of Isabella.

"Your daughter is beautiful! What is her name?" Irini cannot help but stare as her mind puzzles over the déjà-vu of this child.

"Thank you. It's Eva," Jessica beams.

"Okay, Jessica, are your parents survivors of the war?" Irini wants to understand the connection. Her brain is still processing how Jessica's child resembles Bella.

"No. But what you write about family legacies—well, I can relate to the lies, the cheating, and the dishonesty," Jessica smiles knowingly.

"Yes," Irini affirms. She feels troubled by Jessica's tone. Irini's analytical mind sleuths details, including the vivid memories that helped her write her memoir about family betrayal. She stares searchingly into Eva's eyes.

"And your husband is Paul, right?" Jessica leads. She feels she has nothing to lose.

The little girl utters, "Papa." It was a cute moniker for 'Daddy' that stuck when Eva began stringing sounds together.

Irini's blood runs cold, and her pen freezes above the page. *All the pieces fit. Cassandra had not been a match. Bella received stem cells from an unknown donor whose umbilical cord blood matched perfectly. Irini never questioned it; she was so relieved that Bella would survive! This baby, Eva, is about one year old. Bella and Eva are sisters!* Irini feels blindsided! Her relationship, the one she'd tried to do differently, is founded on the same lies. She didn't see this coming, and she feels duped.

"Are you…?" Irini's mind is triaging the pieces: "You donated Eva's cord blood," she deadpans.

"We did—Eva's father and me," Jessica smirks. "Good luck with your book!" She turns away, asking herself why she is so hellbent on twisting the knife into this unsuspecting woman's back. *Is it because Irini gets to keep the guy?* Jessica knows Paul will never leave his wife, and he is already onto his next conquest: a young doctor. *At least he is paying child support. Jessica gets to keep the child. Eva is hers.*

Still trying to grasp all the lies, late nights, missed dinners, and absences, Irini feels her stomach churn with this sucker punch. The bile of deception rises in her throat. Irini wants to vomit as she discovers the only truth that sticks: *Paul and Cassandra!*

Irini hurls the unsigned book; it narrowly misses Eva, clips Jessica's right shoulder blade, and falls to the floor.

Questions for Discussion

1. What is the gift Eva gives? Did you notice any others? If so, what are they?

2. Do you believe Jessica wants to entrap Paul and ruin his marriage and family?

3. Is Paul selfish and self-serving, or does he have a compulsion? How should Paul address his behaviour?

4. Do you think Irini knows Paul is cheating or is she in denial?

5. What might Cassandra have done differently with Irini and Paul regarding Isabella?

6. What double lives did you observe the characters leading?

7. What did you notice about how the characters each cope with their pain?

8. How did the war shape this family?

9. What are the parallels between Cassandra and Irini?

10. How do the female characters change throughout the story?
11. What should Irini do when she discovers the truth?
12. What positive legacies did you notice?
13. Now that you've finished the story, reread the Prologue. What do you believe occurred for Isabella and Eva to share a close bond?
14. Which character(s) do you like and dislike in this story? Why?
15. Do you believe that the actions of our parents and grandparents shape our lives?